Readers' Theatre

By
Judy Truesdell Mecca

Incentive Publications
Nashville, Tennessee

Illustrated by Kris Sexton
Cover by Angela Stiff
Edited by Jill Norris
Copy edited by Cary Grayson

ISBN 0-86530-031-3

1   2   3   4   5   6   7   8   9   10   09   08   07   06

PRINTED IN THE UNITED STATES OF AMERICA
www.incentivepublications.com

Why Readers' Theatre?

Readers' theatre does not rely on costumes, lighting, scenery, props, or sound and music effects. In Readers' Theatre, readers, using primarily their voices, interpret a script—they tell the story. Striving for fluent, expressive reading, your students will pay attention to punctuation and sentence structure as they read aloud. They will enlarge their vocabularies. They will articulate unfamiliar words that may come from another time or place. They will understand and communicate the theme to their audience. Reading aloud, students will sharpen their communication skills. They learn to project their voices and the emotions behind the writing. They discover the values of pacing and inflection. They practice quick response to other readers. Even the shyest, most reluctant reader is part of a group effort in sharing a story with an expectant audience.

It's as easy as one, two, three.

1. Choose and prepare the script. You will need one script for each reader so that lines can be highlighted and stage directions noted. Locate the simple props that will be needed.

2. Introduce the vocabulary, give a brief summary of the action, and choose the cast.

3. Review the script with students and then have students practice reading the script together. Watch your students blossom as confident, fluent readers!

Table of Contents

A Note from the Author about Readers' Theatre

"Do I have to read out loud?"

"I hate to be the one to have to read in class . . . "

"Oh, no. I'm the slowest reader in our room."

Have you heard your students saying things like this?

One of our ongoing goals at Incentive Publications is the continuing pursuit of reading mastery. Not only do we want America's young people to read fluently, understand, and retain what they've read, we want them to enjoy it and realize what a tool it is for the rest of their lives. The better readers they become, the more easily realized is this goal.

Presenting *Readers' Theatre*, a collection of plays meant to be read aloud. This is a different form of theatrical presentation than we've offered teachers and group leaders in the past. Students read these plays aloud without scenery or props or costumes—or memorization. Students typically sit in their acting area (which can be an auditorium stage, a classroom—or the hall!), usually on stools so that they're positioned a little higher and are more easily seen. Students have copies of the play in binders positioned in front of them, typically on music stands. The acting challenge for each student is to convey emotion, humor, plot, and characterization utilizing only the voice, the face, and the upper body. The reading challenge is to become so familiar with the lines that the students stop dreading reading aloud, and indeed look forward to the opportunity to entertain, be silly, talk in a different voice—to take part in readers' theatre.

These plays offer varying levels of reading (and acting) challenges. Though the book is intended for middle school students, your students may wish to perform some of the plays for younger audiences. *Three Bears and Three Goats*, for instance, is a more humorous version of the two fairy tales, knitted together with a narrator. *In the City Where I Live* is another play which may be suitable for entertaining a younger group of boys and girls. Other plays, such as *At The Fence*, deal with issues of friendship and loyalty and will offer an acting challenge to boys and girls who really want to flex their Thespian muscles. *Sounds of Halloween* provides an opportunity for some creative voice work, and K-Zoo Radio, *The Great Science Fair Tragedy*, and *Big Game, Little Guy* are just fun and funny—with increased fluency as an added attraction.

In most of the scripts, there are opportunities to include as many boys and girls as would like to participate. For instance, in *The Great Science Fair Tragedy*, the Chorus can be as large or small as you like—and it is one of the most important parts of this play based on the structure of ancient Greek plays. The Ghostly Chorus in *Sounds of Halloween* can also be expanded, as well as the Cheerleaders and Football Team Members in *Big Game, Little Guy*.

We've modified tradition in a few of the plays. For instance, it isn't customary for readers' theatre actors to turn to each other; they continually face the audience. In one or two of the plays, we do have the actors speaking to each other, then to the audience. They should give the suggestion of speaking to each other, rather than turning to fully face their fellow cast members. Most of their face should be visible at all times. Also, though props or make-up aren't typically employed in readers' theatre, there are a couple of places where, for instance, real chains can be used to create ghostly chain noises, or blocks of wood call to mind goats tripping across the bridge. And if your animal-actors want to experiment with a little make-up or maybe a headdress in the play that takes place in the zoo—it is doubtful that anyone will seriously object.

Have a wonderful time with these light-hearted plays written with your junior high/middle school students in mind. We predict that, before long, you'll be hearing:

"Can we work on our play today? Please? I'll read first!"

Three Bears
and Three Goats

Readers

Narrator

Wee Tiny Gruff

Moderately Proportioned
Gruff

Mondo Gruff

Jelly Troll

Big Daddy Bear

YoYo Mama Bear

Preschool Bear

Goldilocks

Three Bears and Three Goats

Notes to the Teacher / Director:

Here is a combination of two beloved fairy tales, *The Three Billy Goats Gruff* and *Goldilocks and the Three Bears*. Updated—and made just a bit sillier—this version is sure to delight audiences of all ages. (You may wish to consider performing this play for elementary school audiences, either on their campus or yours, or even inviting day-care or preschool boys and girls to attend.)

In addition to the customary readers' theatre stools and music stands, you'll need three bells—one small with a small sound, one a little larger and louder, and one big, noisy bell such as a cowbell. You'll also need three pairs of wooden blocks for the Goats to knock together as they walk across the bridge. Later, Goldilocks will use one pair to make the sound of knocking at the door of the Bears' home.

Before beginning rehearsals, you may wish to discuss the following words or phrases that may be challenging or new to your cast:

- Moderately Proportioned Gruff
- magnificent
- Schwarzenegger
- Bermuda
- résumé
- Jalapeño peppers
- assembling

- arranging
- expressive
- menacing
- reputation
- touché
- allergic

Have fun with characterizations and voices in these plays. Big Daddy Bear, for instance, should have a cool, mellow voice that brings to mind the beret-wearing beatniks of jazz eras gone by. Jelly Troll should, of course, have a growly . . . well, *troll* voice, and the goats should have voices matching their sizes.

In the *Three Bears* portion of the play, a reference is made to Playstation 2, with a note to "Insert current coveted fad here." Have your cast decide the definitive possession that would cause Preschool Bear to welcome Goldilocks into their group immediately.

Have fun, and remember . . . good things come in threes!

(On stage are four stools, with a fifth to the side. The NARRATOR is seated on the stool to the side; the THREE GOATS GRUFF and the TROLL are on the other four. There are music stands in front of them on which their scripts rest, in notebooks. Each GOAT has a pair of wood blocks and a bell. They open their script-books together, and the NARRATOR begins reading.)

NARRATOR   Hello ladies and gentlemen, and welcome to our readers' theatre production, *Three Bears and Three Goats*. We thank you for taking off work, arranging a baby sitter, or whatever you had to do to be with us today!

Let me tell you a little bit about readers' theatre, in case this is your first readers' theatre play ever to see in your whole life. We actors . . .

CAST   *(Throwing up their hands, bowing, etc.)* Ta da!!!

NARRATOR   . . . will be acting out two well-known and well-loved fairy tales for your pleasure today. Only, we will be sitting on stools, using only our voices . . .

WEE TINY GRUFF   Magnificent voices that they are!

NARRATOR   . . . and our faces . . .

MODERATELY PROPORTIONED GRUFF   Attractive faces, indeed!

NARRATOR   Some more than others . . .

MODERATELY PROPORTIONED GRUFF   Hey!

NARRATOR   and our expressive hands and upper bodies . . .

MONDO GRUFF   I'll say they're expressive . . . oh no, I'm upset! *(He pantomimes flailing his hands all around as though showing distress.)* And now I'm worried! *(Wringing hands and cringing)* But now I'm happy! *(Throwing up his arms and stretching hands out wide to show a very happy GOAT)*

NARRATOR   There's a difference between being expressive and being a ham.

MONDO GRUFF   *(To his fellow actors)* Who's he calling a ham? I'm a goat, not a pig! The very idea!

NARRATOR   Anyway . . . you're about to enjoy a different kind of theatre than you usually see . . . we hope you enjoy it!

JELLY TROLL   Say, can we get on with things? My mind's starting to wander.

NARRATOR   Yes, Jelly Troll, we can begin.

JELLY TROLL   Thank you.

NARRATOR   Once upon a time, there were three billy goats called Gruff.

WEE TINY GRUFF   *(Raising his hand)* I have a question.

NARRATOR   Wee Tiny Gruff?

WEE TINY GRUFF   Yes. I want to know why they were all called Gruff. I mean, weren't there enough names to go around in those days?

NARRATOR   Well . . . I guess it was their last name, like Smith or Jones or Schwarzennegger.

MODERATELY PROPORTIONED GRUFF   I always thought it had to do with the fact that they were gruff. You know, like they had bad tempers.

NARRATOR   I honestly never thought about it. May we continue?

MONDO GRUFF   I'm insulted that someone would think that I'm gruff. I'm a gentle soul . . .

JELLY TROLL   All right, already! Who cares why they were all called "gruff"? Let's just do the play.

WEE TINY GRUFF   Jelly Troll, for someone named after a pastry, you aren't very sweet.

NARRATOR   Once upon a time, in a hilly country with lots of lush green meadows, there lived three billy goats . . . who happened to share the last name of "Gruff."

WEE TINY GRUFF   I still wonder why.

NARRATOR   When spring came . . . *(The GOATS GRUFF all start to make bird chirping sounds.)* . . . they wished that they could go up the side of Mount Bermuda and eat the green, sweet grass they had heard was there. The only problem was . . . *(GOATS make "Dun, da dun dun" menacing music sounds.)* . . . there was a bridge they had to cross in order to get to Mount Bermuda, and a mean old troll lived under it.

MODERATELY PROPORTIONED GRUFF	I wonder why he lived *under* the bridge. Why not on top of it, or beside it in a little tent?
NARRATOR	I supposed he wanted to hide his gross ugliness from the world.
JELLY TROLL	OK, now, this is just getting cruel. I am a troll, and trolls are not generally considered handsome . . .
MONDO GRUFF	Except for *Shrek II* when Shrek gets enchanted and becomes like a handsome man for a while.
JELLY TROLL	I knew I was going to hear the name Shrek before we even got three pages into this play. And, for your information, Shrek was an ogre, not a troll.
MONDO GRUFF	I thought he was a troll! All this time I've been comparing the two of you.
NARRATOR	And so . . . *(Looking menacingly at his actors who smile and look innocent)* . . . one spring they decided that they would gather their courage and head for Mount Bermuda, even if they had to face the evil troll.
JELLY TROLL	Oh, so now I'm evil.
CAST	Shhhh!
NARRATOR	And so they discussed who would go first . . .
MONDO GRUFF	My fellow Goats Gruff, I think we all agree that it's time we stand up to that troll and try to make our way to the green pastures of Mount Bermuda.
MODERATELY PROPORTIONED GRUFF	I've heard that the grass there is as green as you can imagine.
WEE TINY GRUFF	I've heard that it's as green as all the green crayons in a 64-crayon box!
ALL GOATS	*(With awe and wonder)* Wow.
MONDO GRUFF	I don't think it would be wise if we all try to go together. The troll will hear us for sure.
MODERATELY PROPORTIONED GRUFF	Maybe we should take turns and see if one of us can sneak over the bridge.

MONDO GRUFF	That might work.
WEE TINY GRUFF	I have a better idea. I'm the smallest goat . . .
MODERATELY PROPORTIONED GRUFF	Yes, Wee Tiny Gruff, you are.
WEE TINY GRUFF	So, let me go first! I'll tippy-toe over the bridge quiet as a mouse. When I get to the other side, Moderately Proportioned Gruff can follow!
MONDO GRUFF	It's worth a try.
WEE TINY GRUFF	I'm off! If I don't come back soon, you come after me, Moderately Proportioned Gruff. I'll either be safe and sound on the other side, or I'll be . . . you know . . . toast.
ANNOUNCER	With that, Wee Tiny Gruff put his head down, his chest out, and headed for the bridge that crossed over the river.
WEE TINY GRUFF	Here I go . . . almost there . . .
ANNOUNCER	Wee Tiny Gruff reached the bridge and began to cross. Cloppity clop went his little hooves *(WEE TINY GRUFF knocks his wooden blocks together lightly.)* and ring-a-ling *(WEE TINY GRUFF rings his little bell.)* went the little bell around his neck. Then, all at once . . .
JELLY TROLL	Who's that trotting over my bridge?
WEE TINY GRUFF	*(Aside)* Busted! *(To JELLY TROLL)* Why, I'm . . . er . . . I'm an art student at the local university, and I'm just going up to Mount Bermuda to draw a sketch.
JELLY TROLL	Oh, an art student! Why didn't you say so . . . wait a minute . . . where is your sketch pad? Where are your pencils or charcoals? I think you're one of the Billy Goats Gruff and you want to go up to the mountain to eat the good green grass there!
WEE TINY GRUFF	What? That's ridiculous! I'm just . . . that is . . . well, you've got me. That's exactly where I'm headed, and that's exactly the reason.
JELLY TROLL	So sorry to mess up your plans, but I think I'm going to eat a little goat for my breakfast!

WEE TINY GRUFF Let me throw out this other suggestion. There's another goat who is coming along right after me. He is much bigger and juicier than I, and would make a much better breakfast.

JELLY TROLL Hmmm . . . a larger, juicier goat . . . that might be worth waiting for.

WEE TINY GRUFF Even if he doesn't show up, if you let me get to Mount Bermuda to eat, I'll be much fatter by the time you next see me. It's a win-win situation.

JELLY TROLL Oh, all right—but be quick about it! Make no mistake—if the other goat doesn't come along, I'm coming after you!

WEE TINY GRUFF Don't worry! He'll be here!

NARRATOR And he ran up the hill and to the green meadow where he feasted on the delicious grass. Meanwhile, the others were getting concerned . . .

MONDO GRUFF *(pantomiming looking at watch)* Wee Tiny Gruff isn't back yet. I wonder if he made it to the other side?

MODERATELY PROPORTIONED GRUFF I don't know—but I'll go find out. Wish me luck!

MONDO GRUFF Good luck! I'll come after you if I don't see you soon.

NARRATOR So Moderately Pro . . . *(acting as if he is too tired to say this long name)* . . . the middle-sized goat . . . headed for the bridge, and began to clop-clop over. *(MODERATELY PROPORTIONED GRUFF taps his blocks together a little more loudly than WEE TINY GRUFF did.)* The slightly larger bell around his neck rang as he walked. *(He rings his slightly larger bell.)*

MODERATELY PROPORTIONED GRUFF Now, why didn't I think to leave this bell at home! I think I'll just sneak it from around my neck and throw it into the . . .

JELLY TROLL Who's that stamping across my bridge ringing that bell loudly enough to wake the dead?

MODERATELY PROPORTIONED GRUFF See? I shoulda' left the bell at home. Why do we never think of these things until it's too late? Twenty-twenty hindsight!

JELLY TROLL Answer me! Who goes there?

MODERATELY PROPORTIONED GRUFF *(In a high, scared voice)* It is I . . . *(Clearing his throat and trying to sound braver)* It is I, Moderately Proportioned Gruff . . .

Readers' Theatre

JELLY TROLL	Why are all thee of y'all named Gruff?
MODERATELY PROPORTIONED GRUFF	You know, that's funny. We were just talking about that! We were wondering if they ran out of last names or what!
JELLY TROLL	You're not brothers?
MODERATELY PROPORTIONED GRUFF	No! No relation.
JELLY TROLL	Huh. I guess it's just one of those things. Anyway—whatever your name is, I'm going to eat you for my breakfast . . . or I guess "brunch" is more like it, as late as it's getting!
MODERATELY PROPORTIONED GRUFF	You know, you could eat me right up. But then, within, oh I'd say . . . an hour or so, you'll be hungry again.
JELLY TROLL	Are you commenting on the size of my stomach??
MODERATELY PROPORTIONED GRUFF	I just meant that a much larger goat than myself . . . in fact, we call him Mondo Gruff . . . will be along any minute. Now, you chow down to *that* plate of cabrito, and you'll think you've been at the all-you-can-eat Monday night buffet!
JELLY TROLL	Hmmm. He's bigger than you, you say?
MODERATELY PROPORTIONED GRUFF	Is a Hummer bigger than a MINI Cooper?

(Or insert your favorite large and small cars here.)

JELLY TROLL	What are you talking about? What's a Hummer?
MODERATELY PROPORTIONED GRUFF	Never you mind. Just let me cross over to the fields full of green grass, and I promise you'll see a four-course dinner walking along any minute.
JELLY TROLL	Oh, all right. But if I don't see any gigantic goat in ten minutes, I'm coming to find you and that pipsqueak goat as well! There won't be anything left of you but a smile and a smart remark. Now get going!
MODERATELY PROPORTIONED GRUFF	You don't have to tell me twice!
NARRATOR	So MPG hurried off to join Wee Tiny, and Mondo Gruff began to pace.

MONDO GRUFF   I wonder what has happened! Did they both make it safely across? I'll bet they did. They're probably tossing a nice salad right about now with all that fresh green grass from the meadow. I'm here, pacing and starving to death . . . and they're getting green stains on their hooves from the grass. That's it . . . I'm going after them.

NARRATOR   So Mondo Gruff started out for the bridge. The more he walked, the more angry he became.

MONDO GRUFF   Isn't that just the way it always goes? I stay behind, I take care of things . . . and the two of them go running off, leaving me in their dust, and eating all the food! And why—just because I'm the biggest! What sense does that make? I'm crossing that bridge and no troll better get in my way!

NARRATOR   So Mondo Gruff stormed over the bridge, not caring how much noise his hooves made *(clapping his blocks together loudly)* nor how much noise the big bell around his neck made! *(He rings his bell loudly.)* Of course the troll heard him and popped out.

JELLY TROLL   Who's that stomping over my bridge as though he's mad at his two friends?

MONDO GRUFF   It's me, Mondo Gruff, that's who! Who dares to ask?

JELLY TROLL   What? Who dares to ask? *(Sounding puzzled)* Why, no one's ever asked me a question before. *(Regaining his toughness)* It is I, Jelly Troll, the troll who lives under this bridge.

MONDO GRUFF   What? You're the big bad troll everyone's always talking about in whispers? You don't look so scary to me! In fact, I think I'll just walk right by you and get on over to those spring meadows. I'm hungry.

JELLY TROLL   You're hungry?! Think of me! Two goats, smaller than yourself, have trotted over this bridge today, making me think of goat cheese and other delicacies, and yet I have not had a bite to eat! I might just make a sandwich out of you!

MONDO GRUFF   Oh wait—this is great. You're going to make a sandwich out of me. I certainly don't think so, my grizzled friend. I am hungry, I am big and fierce, and I am in a bad mood because I'm afraid there won't be any grass left when I get to the meadow. Now you have two choices. You can get out of my way, or you can jump down into the river below, never to be heard from again. Which will it be, your trollness?

JELLY TROLL Well—I really don't want to jump down into the river. I never learned to swim and I really hate bugs. But I can't just let you pass! What kind of a troll lets three goats cross his bridge in one day?

MONDO GRUFF I guess a troll with the goofy name of "Jelly Troll," that's who.

JELLY TROLL This just isn't going to look good on my resume. My reputation is at stake.

MONDO GRUFF Ok, how about this: What's your favorite kind of food?

JELLY TROLL I like fried goat, shish-kebab goat, poached goat, blackened goat . . .

MONDO GRUFF Besides goat.

JELLY TROLL Barbecue.

MONDO GRUFF Barbecue? Really?

JELLY TROLL Yes. I like the real kind, not the kind they make with mustard.

MONDO GRUFF Well, it just so happens that there's a restaurant called Outlaw's Barbecue just on the other side of Mount Bermuda.

JELLY TROLL You are kidding me! How could I not have known this?

MONDO GRUFF I got a coupon from them just the other day, but I ate it because we have no grass on this side of the hill. However, if you'll promise to behave and not eat my friends or me, I'll even give you a ride to the other side of Mount Bermuda. What do you say? Hop on!

JELLY TROLL Really? You'd give me a ride to the barbecue place?

MONDO GRUFF Yes, troll, but this is a limited time offer. Hop on or miss the boat . . . er, goat.

NARRATOR So Jelly Troll hopped on the back of Mondo Gruff, and together they trotted over to Mount Bermuda where the other two goats were almost full.

WEE TINY GRUFF   Thank goodness you're here, Mondo Gruff! Come eat some of this patch right here. I'm stuffed!

MODERATELY PROPORTIONED GRUFF   Oh no, come this way Mondo Gruff! This is wonderful grass over here! It's light, yet full bodied! You'll love it!

NARRATOR   As for the troll . . . did you think that Mondo Gruff was making up the barbecue restaurant? Did you think that he was tricking the troll to let him cross? Clap your hands if that's what you thought!

(Audience claps.)

Sorry! You are mistaken. However—you just saved Tinker Bell. Believe it or not, there really was an entire food court on the other side of the mountain, with Outlaw's Barbecue, a Sonic, and Paradise Bakery. The troll had never ventured to that side of the mountain because he was always hovering near the bridge, trying to keep goats and other animals from crossing over. When asked why he had always done this, the troll answered:

JELLY TROLL   I don't know. It's just what a troll is supposed to do. Now, can I have some more ribs?

NARRATOR   The troll dined for the rest of his days on fast food, and, although his cholesterol was high, he lived happily ever after. The goats were, of course, free to come and go as they pleased, but they were sensible and stuck to the fresh, green grass of the meadow. I guess there's supposed to be a moral to this story. Fairy tales have morals, don't they?

GOATS & JELLY TROLL   Don't be eating goats, because they may know the way to the barbecue.

NARRATOR   Works for me. How about a nice hand for the cast of this part of our play!

(Audience applauds.)

Thank you. At this time, the actors will prepare to play their roles in the next portion of our presentation which involves three bears!

(The actors get off of their stools and run around the acting area,
then take their seats again, perhaps on different stools.)

Readers' Theatre

NARRATOR	This portion of our play involves three bears who were jazz musicians . . . Big Daddy Bear . . .
BIG DADDY BEAR	What's up? Be cool, y'all.
NARRATOR	Big Daddy Bear played the saxophone.
BIG DADDY BEAR	Nothing beats the sweet sound of straight-ahead jazz.
NARRATOR	Yoyo Mama Bear . . .
YOYO MAMA BEAR	Hello, everyone! I play the jazz cello.
NARRATOR	Hmmm. I've never heard of jazz cello.
YOYO MAMA BEAR	I had never heard of readers' theatre before today!
NARRATOR	Touché!
PRESCHOOL BEAR	Don't forget me!
NARRATOR	Oh, of course . . . and Preschool Bear.
PRESCHOOL BEAR	I play drums a little. But mostly I play with blocks and Army men. I used to be called "Baby Bear," but then I learned my shapes and colors.
NARRATOR	One sunny summer day, Yoyo Mama Bear made the family a large pot of porridge.
BIG DADDY BEAR	Yum, Yoyo Mama Bear, I do love mellow porridge.
YOYO MAMA BEAR	Well I'm glad you do, Big Daddy Bear, because that's all I'm fixing for lunch today!
BIG DADDY BEAR	That's all I need—if you've got some sweet honey and cinnamon to top it off!
YOYO MAMA BEAR	I surely do! I know what a sweet tooth you have!
NARRATOR	She served Big Daddy his porridge, and he sprinkled the top with cinnamon and honey.
BIG DADDY BEAR	It smells delicious!
NARRATOR	Yoyo Mama Bear put some porridge in her own bowl . . .

YOYO MAMA BEAR   Sometimes I like honey and cinnamon on my porridge too, but today I'm in a different mood. I'm thinking . . . picante sauce with jalapeño peppers.

NARRATOR   Yoyo Mama Bear was in a spicy mood! She served Preschool Bear his porridge, and he wanted something else . . .

PRESCHOOL BEAR   I want chocolate chips. I want chocolate chips on everything! I would wear chocolate-chip clothes if they made them! I wish I could drive a chocolate-chip car!

NARRATOR   Preschool Bear sometimes got carried away. Anyway, Yoyo Mama Bear served up the porridge, and everyone started to dig in . . .

ALL THREE BEARS   Yow! It's too hot to eat!

NARRATOR   All of your porridge is too hot?

YOYO MAMA BEAR   Yes! I mean, my porridge is supposed to be spicy hot but not temperature hot! I guess I left it in the microwave too long.

BIG DADDY BEAR   Not to worry, Yoyo Mama Bear! Let's just take a little cruise around the 'hood . . .

PRESCHOOL BEAR   He means "a walk."

BIG DADDY BEAR   And while we're out for a stroll, our porridge will become cool. Like us!

YOYO MAMA BEAR   Well, I'm sorry I got the porridge so hot, but a little walk does sound nice.

BIG DADDY BEAR   Then what are we waiting for? Off we go!

NARRATOR   So the three bears left their porridge sitting on the table and went for a little walk in the 'hood. I mean "the woods." *(He looks at the BEARS.)* Pssst . . . go on . . . exit!

THE BEARS   Pssst . . . readers' theatre!

NARRATOR   *(Smacking his forehead as if to say "dumb me!")* Oh, that's right! Sorry!

GOLDILOCKS   Say! Don't forget about me!

Readers' Theatre

NARRATOR	Right! Well . . . while the bears were out walking and enjoying the day . . . *(THE BEARS ad lib snapping their fingers, singing "scat," and generally being cool musicians.)* . . . thank you, bears, that's enough to get the idea across.
(They become quiet.)	A young girl was out in the woods.
GOLDILOCKS	Hello, everybody. I'm a Girl Scout and I'm working on my Explorer badge.
NARRATOR	She had wandered away from the campsite where her troop members had set up their tents.
GOLDILOCKS	This really looks bad. I'm working on my Explorer badge, and yet I've gotten separated from the rest of the girls and I can't find my way back! I've been wandering all morning and I'm really hungry and tired!
NARRATOR	This girl . . . say, what's your name?
GOLDILOCKS	It's the worst. I hate to even say it.
NARRATOR	Go ahead. No one will laugh.
GOLDILOCKS	I don't think they'll laugh. I think they'll feel sorry for me!
NARRATOR	What is it?
GOLDILOCKS	My name . . . is Goldilocks. *(Looks at the audience.)* See! Look at their faces! They pity me. And they should! It's an awful name. I mean, it's OK if I leave my hair blonde, and it curls up—you know, like if it's a humid day. But maybe I don't want to always be a blonde and listen to all those jokes. Maybe I want to have long, straight dark hair—or be a redhead! Can you imagine what that would be like? "Oh, hello, little girl, what's your name?" "Goldilocks." "Goldilocks? Then why is your hair straight and red? Are you color blind?" I can hear it now!
NARRATOR	I'll admit it's an unusual name . . . why do you think your parents named you that?
GOLDILOCKS	Well—my mother's name is Dark Roots, and my father's name is Balding On Top, so I guess they thought it was a fine name.
NARRATOR	I see. Can we get back to the story?

GOLDILOCKS	Please.
NARRATOR	Well—Goldilocks came upon the home of the three bears.
GOLDILOCKS	What's this? A cute little house! Maybe I could ask for a drink of water.
NARRATOR	She knocked on the door . . .
GOLDILOCKS	*(knocking on one of the GOATS' wood blocks)* Hello? Is anybody there? *(She waits a moment, listening.)* Hello? Hmmmm. No one seems to be at home. I think I'll go in anyway. Maybe there's a map of the area and I can find the Girl Scout camp site!
NARRATOR	So Goldilocks tiptoed into the Bears' kitchen . . .
GOLDILOCKS	Oh, look! It's a cozy little kitchen!
NARRATOR	And she spied the porridge bowls.
GOLDILOCKS	What's this? Little bowls of . . . of . . . porridge. *(To NARRATOR)* Say, what is "porridge" anyway?
NARRATOR	I think it's like oatmeal, but not sweet.
GOLDILOCKS	Oh! Good! For some reason, I just don't have a sweet tooth. I know I shouldn't sneak a bite . . . I mean, a Girl Scout is honest . . . but I am SO hungry . . . and there is SO much porridge . . . maybe a tiny bite won't hurt!
NARRATOR	So Goldilocks took a taste of Big Daddy Bear's porridge . . .
GOLDILOCKS	*(Making a noise as if spitting it out)* Yuck! Honey and . . . is that cinnamon? Yuck! Reminds me of the spice cookies we have to sell. Maybe I'll try this one . . .
NARRATOR	She moved to Yoyo Mama Bear's place at the table and took a tiny taste of her porridge . . .
GOLDILOCKS	This bowl looks different . . . I'll just try a taste . . . *(Pantomiming a hot mouth and teary eyes)* Yowee! It's spicy!
NARRATOR	Goldilocks spit the spicy porridge out and looked around for something to drink.
GOLDILOCKS	What? No milk? No water? No Kool-Aid?

NARRATOR	She spied Preschool Bear's porridge bowl next.
GOLDILOCKS	I'm afraid to try this bowl—who knows what's in it! But—here goes . . .
NARRATOR	She took a taste of Preschool Bear's porridge . . .
GOLDILOCKS	Yuck! Chocolate chips! *(Looking around)* How can I get this taste out of my mouth . . . ah! There's the pot of porridge, in its microwave-safe bowl. Maybe it's plain . . . *(She pantomimes tasting it.)* Yum! It's a little warm . . . but it doesn't taste like anything silly! I think I'll eat it all up.
NARRATOR	Goldilocks ate it all up. *(A pause, then:)* Can I say something here?
GOLDILOCKS	Sure, go ahead.
NARRATOR	I'm really glad that all those porridge bowls were different flavors. I've always thought it was weird that the bowls cooled at different rates. I mean, why would one bowl still be too hot, one be too cold, and one be just right? It never made sense to me.
GOLDILOCKS	I'm with you.
NARRATOR	OK, back to the story. After eating all the plain porridge, Goldilocks went from room to room looking for a map that would help her find her campsite.
GOLDILOCKS	I can't believe I wandered off from my troop. I can't expect these people to have a map . . . wait! What's this? A MapQuest print-out!
NARRATOR	Goldilocks was surprised to see that the Bear family had access to the Internet in the woods.
GOLDILOCKS	Now, if I can just figure out this map . . . let's see, here's the fork in the road . . .
NARRATOR	As Goldilocks looked at the computer print-out, she tried to find a place to sit. First she came to Big Daddy's easy chair . . .
GOLDILOCKS	Let's see . . . I'll just sit down here and have a look . . . wahhhh!

NARRATOR	What Goldilocks meant by "wahhhh!" was that the chair was so soft and fluffy that she sank down into the cushions.
GOLDILOCKS	I'm afraid I'll disappear if I sit down in that chair! Maybe this one?
NARRATOR	She sat down on Yoyo Mama Bear's straight-back chair.
GOLDILOCKS	Ouch! This is hard!
NARRATOR	It was the chair on which Yoyo Mama Bear sits when she practices her cello.
GOLDILOCKS	Oh, look at this chair! It's so cute with little ducks and bunnies on it . . .
NARRATOR	Goldilocks tried to sit in Preschool Bear's little chair . . . but it was way too small for her!
GOLDILOCKS	Oh no! Look what I've done! It's broken all to pieces. Can I put it back together? If I had some rope . . . what am I saying? I didn't get my Knot-Tying badge yet. I don't know how to repair a busted-up chair.
NARRATOR	Goldilocks was still lost, and, although she was no longer hungry, she was still very tired. She was trying to understand the MapQuest map when she noticed that there were three nice beds in the corner.
GOLDILOCKS	*(Yawning)* Oh oh, there are some beds. Now I really shouldn't just lie down in one of these beds . . . that would be just rude. I mean, it's one thing to eat their porridge . . . oh my, I shouldn't have done that either. But I was so hungry . . . and I'm so tired . . . I've been trying to retrace my steps for hours . . . maybe I could just lie down for a minute . . . wahhh!
NARRATOR	This time when Goldilocks said "Wahh!", she meant "This is a waterbed, and I'm rocking and rolling all around!"
GOLDILOCKS	This is a waterbed, and I'm . . .
NARRATOR	I've translated already. Move on to the next bed.
GOLDILOCKS	OK, thanks. This one looks nice . . . except that . . . *(Beginning to sneeze)* I think that . . . *achew!* It must have . . . *achew!* . . .

feather pillows and maybe . . . *achew!* . . . a down comforter! I'm so allergic! *Achew!* I should probably have allergy shots . . .

NARRATOR Then Goldilocks spied Preschool Bear's little bed, which was shaped like a race car.

GOLDILOCKS Look at this cute little bed, shaped like a racecar. I bet I could just catch a quick nap and be on my way before these people get back . . .

NARRATOR With that, she fell asleep, all tucked down in Preschool Bear's little bed. Pretty soon . . . you guessed it . . . the Bear family returned.

BIG DADDY BEAR That was a groovin' walk, dears! Now I really have an appetite for my lunch!

PRESCHOOL BEAR So do I, Big Daddy! I can't wait to eat . . . say! Look at this!

YOYO MAMA BEAR Why, what on earth? It looks like someone's been in our kitchen tasting our porridge!

BIG DADDY BEAR I should've set the alarm.

YOYO MAMA BEAR We were only gone for a minute. Oh, well—I'll get some more porridge for us. What's this? The bowl is empty!

PRESCHOOL BEAR I'm scared! What if it's a monster, and he's in the house somewhere?

BIG DADDY BEAR I'm pretty sure monsters don't eat porridge, son. But let's walk through the house and make sure.

PRESCHOOL BEAR If you say so . . .

BIG DADDY BEAR We'll start with the living room.

YOYO MAMA BEAR Why, look at that! Our chairs look fine, but Preschool Bear's little chair is broken to bits!

BIG DADDY BEAR Now I'm starting to lose my cool. Who would invade our mellow space and bust up our furniture?

PRESCHOOL BEAR Big Daddy Bear! Yoyo Mama Bear! Look in my bed!

NARRATOR The three bears rushed into the corner where the beds were kept.

PRESCHOOL BEAR	Look in my bed! It's a little girl!
GOLDILOCKS	*(Drowsily, just waking up)* I'm not little! I'm a Junior Girl Scout.
YOYO MAMA BEAR	What are you doing in our son's bed, child?
BIG DADDY BEAR	Are you the one who made toothpicks out of my son's chair?
GOLDILOCKS	*(Now fully awake and scared)* Oh, yes! I'm the one. I'm so sorry! I was just trying to find my way back to my campsite . . .
YOYO MAMA BEAR	Well, why didn't you just wait for us? We would've helped you find your way!
BIG DADDY BEAR	Is it Camp Tiger Woods?
GOLDILOCKS	Yes! Do you know it?
BIG DADDY BEAR	Why yes, my young friend! Our cool jazz band played a concert 'round the campfire just last week!
GOLDILOCKS	Concert?! Jazz band?! I'm a singer!
YOYO MAMA BEAR	We've been looking for a vocalist! Can you sing scat?
GOLDILOCKS	*(Singing)* Shoo-be-doop-bop-do-wah!
BIG DADDY BEAR	You sound groovin'!
GOLDILOCKS	Maybe I can get my Musician badge in Girl Scouts!
PRESCHOOL BEAR	Hey, wait a minute! This girl ate up our porridge, broke my chair, and took a nap in my bed! And now you're inviting her into our group!
GOLDILOCKS	I have a PlayStation 2 *(or insert current coveted fad)*.
PRESCHOOL BEAR	Welcome to the family!
BIG DADDY BEAR	We need to think of a name for our group.
GOLDILOCKS	How about "Blondie"?
YOYO MAMA BEAR	Too "eighties."
GOLDILOCKS	"The Chicago Cubs"?

Readers' Theatre

BIG DADDY BEAR Too sporty.

PRESCHOOL BEAR How about "Goldilocks and the Three Bears"?

ALL Goldilocks and the Three Bears?

PRESCHOOL BEAR Yes!

ALL *(A pause, then:)* Not catchy enough.

PRESCHOOL BEAR Nobody listens to me!

(The CAST starts ad-libbing about what their name could be and when they could rehearse.)

NARRATOR So the Bear family guided Goldilocks back to Camp Tiger Woods. In the days that followed, she got her Explorer badge, as well as her Musician's badge, her Porridge Cooking badge, and her Chair Re-Assembling badge. You know, there had to be some penalty for breaking, entering, and eating. But they became great friends, sang at various campfires around the forest, and now they say to you, our wonderful audience:

CAST Thank you for coming to our readers' theatre play!

(They all wave goodbye.)

Three Bears and Three Goats

Follow-up Activities

1. If you host a performance of this play at your school, create a publicity crew from within your cast or classroom to write press releases and send them to your local paper. What else could the publicity crew (sometimes called "House and Pub" in college theatre departments) do to promote the performance? Could they create posters for local businesses and your middle school hallways? Ushers will be needed to hand out programs; they might want to consider dressing up as fairy tale characters. Artistic class or cast members could be pressed into service to create programs by hand or by computer.

2. You might also consider a performance for a local facility which cares for the elderly—they might be just as enchanted to hear these familiar stories as the little ones! As a cast, decide what would be different about a performance for senior citizens. How could you ensure the maximum enjoyment for these folks? Discuss why it might be a good idea to travel to them rather than to invite them to your school.

3. Even though these plays are based on fairy tales, there are some lessons hidden within. As a class, discuss the mistakes made by characters in each play. For instance, perhaps Mondo Gruff would not have been discovered crossing the bridge if he had not been angry and stomping. Discuss events in your cast members' lives which were made worse by letting their anger cloud their judgment. What about Goldilocks? In today's world, is it a good idea to enter the homes of others, even if they seem deserted?

4. Goldilocks is a Girl Scout in our play, and working on some badges that surely don't exist in real life. Have you ever seen a Chair Re-Assembling badge, or a Porridge Cooking badge? Probably not! Just for fun, think of five badges that you wish would be available for Girl Scouts or Boy Scouts, and design them. Would you like to see a TV Watching badge? How about a Mall Shopping badge? Or one for Skateboarding? Use map colors or markers to create the artwork on these fictitious badges.

5. Write and perform a brief scene (or "sketch") in which The Bears and their new vocalist, Goldilocks, are being interviewed by a talk show host. Who would be cool? Who would be nervous? What would the talk show host's name be? What would be the name of their new CD?

K-ZOO RADIO

Readers

Animal Chorus

Mad Mike
the Morning Monkey

Sheila the Sidekick Seal

Peter the Penguin

Zeke the Zebra

Ellie the Elephant

Baldy the Eagle

The Peacocks

Cameron the Camel

Gary the Groundhog

Paul the Polar Bear

K-Zoo Radio

Notes to the Teacher / Director:

Here is a fast-paced, very silly readers' theatre offering for your students who have fairly solid reading skills—or would like to improve! It's *Radio K-Zoo*, the cool radio station by animals, for animals, broadcasting live from the local zoo. Mad Mike the Morning Monkey does his best to keep control of the morning show, but pretty soon, it's out of his hands—or is it "paws"?

After assigning parts, you may wish to suggest that your young actors listen to morning radio at home or on their way to school to get a feel for how radio personalities speak. There's a certain (sometimes annoying) rhythm and upbeat way of communicating which will be fun to emulate.

There is room for flexibility in casting your Animal Chorus and the Peacocks. The only job the Animal Chorus has is to do the little radio jingle, a combination of singing, speaking, and roaring. You may wish to assign a group of students to be the Animal Chorus, or it could be made up of other cast members with other speaking roles. It can be as large or small as you wish. The same is true for the Peacocks who sing the seemingly never-ending "*On The First Day of Summer*" This group can be any number of singers, and it can also be comprised of actors playing other parts.

You may wish to discuss the pronunciation and meaning of each of the following words before you begin rehearsal:

• sidekick	• reasonable	• colliding	• accurate
• society	• interrupt	• canteen	• reliable
• incorrigible	• concrete	• microfiber	• habitat
• tuxedo	• occasional	• snorting	• mascara
• misbehaved	• concession	• security	• complimentary

Finally, although this is readers' theatre and no costumes or scenery are typically utilized, the theatre police will probably not arrest anyone if your cast wishes to use a bit of stage make-up or fake noses, whiskers, etc., to make their faces look a bit like the animals they portray. You may also wish to have Mike and Sheila wear headphones throughout, with the other actors adding headphones when it is their turn to speak.

Have a roaring good time and remember—it's a zoo out there!

(Stools with chairs and music stands are in place in the acting area. Actors are seated on their stools as the play begins. If you have a way to have music playing as the guests enter, it might be fun to have a song such as "At The Zoo" by Simon and Garfunkel. If you have music, it fades as CAST sings:)

ANIMAL CHORUS   *(Singing at first)* STARTIN' OFF YOUR MORNING WITH A ROAR *(Making roaring sounds)*! K-Z-O-O—ZANY K-ZOO! *(Spoken)* We're all animals!

MAD MIKE THE MORNING MONKEY   And it's a good-looking kind of a Wednesday *(or insert day of performance)* morning here at the Marsalis *(or insert name of town)* Zoo! This is your morning DJ, the sunny voice of the early dawn, the man with a plan with a banana in his hand, Mad Mike the Morning Monkey!

SHEILA THE SIDEKICK SEAL   Good morning, Mad Mike! It's time to talk to the animals!

MAD MIKE THE MORNING MONKEY   It is indeed! As always, it's a pleasure to welcome my loyal and trusty co-star, Sheila the Sidekick Seal!

SHEILA THE SIDEKICK SEAL   That's my name, don't wear it out . . . I may need it to sign checks when I go shopping for fish!

MAD MIKE THE MORNING MONKEY   Ooooh, all you fishes better run and hide. Sheila looks hungry to me!

SHEILA THE SIDEKICK SEAL   I was hungry until I saw that bowl of mush you're eating. What is that, Malto-Gruel?

MAD MIKE THE MORNING MONKEY   It's a little breakfast of mashed-up bananas, if you must know.

SHEILA THE SIDEKICK SEAL   Why, oh why, did I bring it up? Say, Mike, did you do anything fun over the weekend?

MAD MIKE THE MORNING MONKEY   How good of you to ask!

SHEILA THE SIDEKICK SEAL   My pleasure.

MAD MIKE THE MORNING MONKEY   I guess that's why they pay you the big sidekick dollars! Anyway, I was out and about in K-ZOO land, and I attended the grand opening of the new reptile house. Here to report about the big event is our society reporter, Peter the Penguin.

PETER THE PENGUIN   Good morning, good morning, good morning.

SHEILA THE SIDEKICK SEAL   Hey, Peter. You're all dressed up today!

MAD MIKE THE MORNING MONKEY   You sure are! Our morning show is classy, but I don't think it calls for tux and tails!

Readers' Theatre

PETER THE PENGUIN Oh, you two! You're just incorrigible. I'm in my tuxedo for two reasons: One is—I'm just now getting home from the big reptile house grand-opening party. It was such a happening! Everyone was there—Larry and Lucy Lion and their cubs, who misbehaved and knocked over the punch bowl. Sometimes I wonder what parents are thinking. I mean, if the little beasts can't behave, for heaven's sake, hire a sitter and leave them at home! Sally the Stork cub-sits for very reasonable prices . . .

SHEILA THE SIDEKICK SEAL I hate to interrupt you, Peter, but I heard that Sally met with an untimely fate when she was cub-sitting for Terry and Teeny Tiger . . .

MAD MIKE THE MORNING MONKEY I heard about that! It seems the Tiger cubs woke up in the night, hungry for a snack . . . and there was Sally!

PETER THE PENGUIN Oh stop stop stop! Say it isn't so?!

MAD MIKE THE MORNING MONKEY

and **SHEILA THE SIDEKICK SEAL** It isn't so.

PETER THE PENGUIN I repeat—you two are incorrigible.

MAD MIKE THE MORNING MONKEY What does "incorrigible" even mean?

SHEILA THE SIDEKICK SEAL I don't know, but I bet we're it!

PETER THE PENGUIN Ahem! If you don't mind, could I get back to telling about the grand opening? Thanks ever so. OK—the reptile house was stunning with its concrete floors . . .

MAD MIKE THE MORNING MONKEY The better to rinse off with a hose.

PETER THE PENGUIN And its beautiful brass railings, polished to a sparkling shine.

SHEILA THE SIDEKICK SEAL Soon to be covered with little kid handprints . . .

PETER THE PENGUIN The fruit punch was flowing freely, and there were these delicious little chicken fingers . . . everyone agreed that chicken tastes just like snake.

MAD MIKE THE MORNING MONKEY Why, Peter the Penguin, I believe you just popped a funny.

PETER THE PENGUIN Well, just because I know all about high society doesn't mean I don't appreciate the occasional joke. Anyway—music was provided by the Giraffe Wind Symphony—they played really long oboes. Everyone there danced all night and, as I said, many of us are just heading home as the sun comes up over the elephant cages.

SHEILA THE SIDEKICK SEAL	So what's the other reason?
PETER THE PENGUIN	The other reason what?
SHEILA THE SIDEKICK SEAL	You said you were in a tuxedo for two reasons. Besides the reptile house opening, what was the other one?
PETER THE PENGUIN	Oh. Well, Sheila, duh—I'm a penguin and this is how we look. *(Disgustedly)* Seals!
MAD MIKE THE MORNING MONKEY	We've got traffic and weather coming up next, here on . . .
ANIMAL CHORUS	*(Singing)* K-Z-O-O—ZANY K-ZOO! *(Spoken)* We're all animals!
MAD MIKE THE MORNING MONKEY	But first . . . here's a word from one of our fine sponsors . . .
ZEKE THE ZEBRA	Hey all you monkeys, chimps, and orangutans—are you tired of zoo visitors throwing peanuts into your cage? Would you rather have something else for a change, but don't know how to make the foolish humans understand?
ELLE THE ELEPHANT	We here at Kids R Goobers can help! We've put together a collection of flash cards that will speak your mind for you! Imagine the surprise of a zoo visitor when you hold up a card that says, "Keep the peanuts, would ya? I'd rather have a burger!"
ZEKE THE ZEBRA	They'll be shocked at first—but then they'll run for the concession stand! Especially if you hold up the card that says "I like ketchup with my fries!"
ELLE THE ELEPHANT	Or how about this one: "I'm really trying to watch my weight—how about a nice salad?"
ZEKE THE ZEBRA	Not only are these messages written in clear, easy-to-read capital letters, but we've also included a picture on each card! Don't you worry if your little peanut-thrower doesn't know how to read yet . . . when he sees the card with a big "X" over the peanut and big smiley face next to the pizza, he'll get the idea!
ELLE THE ELEPHANT	No need to shell another peanut! Act now! Operators are standing by. Just call 1-NO-MORE-NUTS. That's One, N-O-M-O-R-E-N-U-T-S.
ZEKE THE ZEBRA	If you call before midnight, we'll throw in complimentary salt, pepper, and oregano. Call now!

Readers' Theatre

MAD MIKE THE MORNING MONKEY	And we're back! Here on . . .
ANIMAL CHORUS	*(Singing)* K-Z-O-O—ZANY K-ZOO! *(Spoken)* We're all animals!
MAD MIKE THE MORNING MONKEY	You're here with Mad Mike the Morning Monkey and beautiful Sheila the Sidekick Seal . . .
SHEILA THE SIDEKICK SEAL	Not so beautiful—I don't have any makeup on. Can't seem to find a good waterproof mascara! And for a seal, that's a problem!
MAD MIKE THE MORNING MONKEY	I hear ya. And speaking of hearing, let's go to our eyes and ears on zoo traffic, Baldy the Eagle. Talk to me, Baldy!
BALDY THE EAGLE	Good morning, Mike and Sheila! I'm talking to you from high above the flamingo cage where traffic is starting to really get snarled. There's a big group of Boy Scouts . . . looks like about three busloads . . . and they were headed eastbound toward the bear habitat. Just then, another group—lots of babies and strollers, must be a day care—rushed in, almost colliding with the Boy Scouts in their hurry to get to the bears. A wheel came off of one of the strollers, and it's broken down in the center lane. Several of the Boy Scouts are trying to help—and a lot of flamingos are rubber-necking, trying to see what's going on. So—it's slow going near the bears and the flamingos! In fact—it's a zoo out there! Back to you, Mike and Sheila!
MAD MIKE THE MORNING MONKEY	Thanks for that update. Be careful out there, everybody! What's your hurry? These animals aren't going anywhere!
SHEILA THE SIDEKICK SEAL	No kidding, everybody, simmer down. Maybe we can help them, Mad Mike.
MAD MIKE THE MORNING MONKEY	How's that, Sheila?
SHEILA THE SIDEKICK SEAL	How about we play a little music? We've been talking all morning and haven't played a song to get everybody's day off to a good start.
MAD MIKE THE MORNING MONKEY	That's a great idea. Here are The Peacocks, singing their new hit . . . *"On The First Day of Summer!"*
THE PEACOCKS	*(To the tune of " THE TWELVE DAYS OF CHRISTMAS")* ON THE FIRST DAY OF SUMMER, WE SA-AW AT THE ZOO A PARTRIDGE IN THE BIRDHOUSE.

36

ON THE SECOND DAY OF SUMMER,
WE SA-AW AT THE ZOO
TWO TURTLEDOVES
AND A PARTRIDGE IN THE BIRDHOUSE.

ON THE THIRD DAY OF SUMMER,
WE SA-AW AT THE ZOO
THREE FRENCH HENS,
TWO TURTLEDOVES,
AND A PARTRIDGE IN THE BIRDHOUSE.

ON THE FOURTH DAY OF SUMMER,
WE SA-AW AT THE ZOO
FOUR CALLING MOMS,
THREE FRENCH HENS,
TWO TURTLEDOVES,
AND A PARTRIDGE IN THE BIRDHOUSE.

ON THE FIFTH DAY OF SUMMER,
WE SA-AW AT THE ZOO
FIVE LION KINGS!
FOUR CALLING MOMS,
THREE FRENCH HENS,
TWO TURTLEDOVES,
AND A PARTRIDGE IN THE BIRDHOUSE.

ON THE SIXTH . . .

MAD MIKE THE MORNING MONKEY OK, OK, we get the idea! Sheesh! We'll be here all day if we wait for them to get finished! Quick, somebody, play a commercial!

CAMERON THE CAMEL Attention, camels! Your world is about to change forever! Are you tired of carrying water in your hump? Do you wish you could use that storage space for something else, like snacks or a road map? Well, wish no more! Help is on its way!

The good folks at Humpty Dumpty Camel Supplies have developed a revolutionary new water storage system. It's called the Can-Do Canteen! That's right! All you do is fill up the 25-gallon canteen at the nearest pond, water fountain, or mirage, then hang it around your neck! Sure, you'll move a little more slowly, but you'll be able to carry more stuff! Lady camels, choose from the jewel-tone canteen, or canteens covered in suede or stylish microfiber. You gentlemen camels will surely prefer rugged leather or manly corduroy.

Readers' Theatre

	That's *Humpty Dumpty Camel Supplies*. We would sell you sand in the desert.
MAD MIKE THE MORNING MONKEY	That sounds like a great product. Before we go to weather, let's check back with our song . . .
THE PEACOCKS	. . . TEN FROGS A LEAPING, NINE HIPPOS SNORTING, . . .
MAD MIKE THE MORNING MONKEY	And it's still going on! It's the world's longest song!
SHEILA THE SIDEKICK SEAL	That song's longer than "MacArthur Park" and "Hey Jude" put together!
MAD MIKE THE MORNING MONKEY	Let's be glad no one ever put "MacArthur Park" and "Hey Jude" together. Right now let's check in with Gary the Groundhog in the K-ZOO weather center. Gary? How are we looking? *(a pause)* Gary? You there, buddy?
GARY THE GROUNDHOG	Oh, sorry Mike! I had to run back inside my house for a minute. You won't believe what happened!
SHEILA THE SIDEKICK SEAL	Try us.
GARY THE GROUNDHOG	Well—when I looked out this morning, it was really sunny, so I decided to come out and take a walk. Then I saw this scary-looking, flat kind of gray guy who looked like a taller, skinnier version of me!
MAD MIKE THE MORNING MONKEY	Dude—that wasn't another guy. It was your shadow!!
GARY THE GROUNDHOG	What? It was my shadow? You mean like in *Peter Pan*?
MAD MIKE THE MORNING MONKEY	Yes! Security is very tight here in K-Zoo land. I'm sure it was your shadow and not a bad guy.
GARY THE GROUNDHOG	Wow! I'm really frosted! You mean, all these years in February when I've come out and gone cowering back inside . . . that was my shadow? Not a ghost or a phantom or an alien?
MAD MIKE THE MORNING MONKEY	No, buddy—just your shadow.
GARY THE GROUNDHOG	That does it. I'm taking karate. I am way too big of a scaredy-cat.
MAD MIKE THE MORNING MONKEY	So—about that weather?
GARY THE GROUNDHOG	Sunny.

MAD MIKE THE MORNING MONKEY	*(A pause, then:)* Sunny? That's it?
GARY THE GROUNDHOG	Well—yes. I looked out . . . it was sunny. The forecast is . . . sunny.
MAD MIKE THE MORNING MONKEY	Gee, I'm so glad we have you, Gary! We would never have figured that out on our own.
GARY THE GROUNDHOG	Happy to be of service.
MAD MIKE THE MORNING MONKEY	Thanks, Gary! We'll check back with you later for more . . . accurate and reliable . . . weather.
GARY THE GROUNDHOG	*(Doing a martial arts war cry)* Kee-yah!
MAD MIKE THE MORNING MONKEY	OK, thanks. Wonder how that song is coming . . .
THE PEACOCKS	TWELVE SNAKES A-BITING, ELEVEN DUCKS A-QUACKING, . . .
SHEILA THE SIDEKICK SEAL	It'll never be over!
MAD MIKE THE MORNING MONKEY	My grandchimps can tell me how it turns out.
SHEILA THE SIDEKICK SEAL	I guess we'd better get to the sports report! I'm excited—we've hired a new guy, and I hear he's kinda cute!
MAD MIKE THE MORNING MONKEY	Oh, Sheila, you are such a flirt! Let's get this new sports guy in here. Paul! Oh, Paul the Polar Bear!
PAUL THE POLAR BEAR	Hey, all you good sports! Especially you, Sheila, you cutie!
SHEILA THE SIDEKICK SEAL	Oh, Paul, don't make me blush!
PAUL THE POLAR BEAR	Speaking of blushing, the Ostriches made the Egrets blush in a fight to the finish over the weekend! Ollie was up to bat for the Ostriches—he looked—he nodded—he smacked it! And it was goodbye, baseball!
MAD MIKE THE MORNING MONKEY	Thanks for that report. And now . . .
PAUL THE POLAR BEAR	Oh, wait, not quite finished. The final score of that baseball game was 7–2, Ostriches! Man, were the feathers flying! I also visited football training camp, and I'm happy to report that the home team, the Coyotes, looked awesomely powerful. I think we're going to have a great season as we do battle against neighboring zoo teams.
MAD MIKE THE MORNING MONKEY	That's great to hear! And now a word from . . .

Readers' Theatre

PAUL THE POLAR BEAR But wait! I didn't tell you about the Prairie Dog junior league girls' soccer team! They gave their all in a match with the Armadillos, and it was no contest! The Prairie Dogs were all over the field . . . scoring goals . . . blocking kicks . . . it was awesome!

SHEILA THE SIDEKICK SEAL I think you're awesome, Paul.

PAUL THE POLAR BEAR Back at 'cha, Sheila! And speaking of "back," the Roadrunners played back-to-back hockey games last night . . .

MAD MIKE THE MORNING MONKEY I think that's enough sport talk for the morning, Paul! Thanks!

PAUL THE POLAR BEAR But wait! There was a big fight on the ice . . .

MAD MIKE THE MORNING MONKEY No, really, that's enough! Thanks!

THE PEACOCKS FOUR CALLING MOMS, THREE FRENCH HENS, . . .

ANIMAL CHORUS *(singing)* K-Z-O-O—ZANY K-ZOO! *(spoken)* We're all animals!

MAD MIKE THE MORNING MONKEY Sheila! Help! I've lost control of this morning show!

THE PEACOCKS TWO TURTLEDOVES, . . .

SHEILA THE SIDEKICK SEAL Mike! Let's get out of here!

MAD MIKE THE MORNING MONKEY Good idea, Sheila! As always, this is Mad Mike the Morning Monkey . . .

SHEILA THE SIDEKICK SEAL And Sheila the Sidekick Seal . . .

MAD MIKE THE MORNING MONKEY Reminding you that . . .

SHEILA AND MIKE It's all happening at the zoo!

THE PEACOCKS AND A PARTRIDGE IN THE BIRDHOUSE.

K-ZOO RADIO

Follow-up Activities

1. Choose a character in the play and write a letter from him or her to a relative in a neighboring zoo. Would he or she complain? What things might annoy him about this zoo? About what things would he or she brag?

2. Form a make-up crew for the play. Design make-up to represent all the animals and show each actor how to apply his or her make-up. Don't forget hair—would Sheila's hair be slicked back? Would the Peacocks have blue make-up on their faces, and a fan of colorful construction paper feathers attached to their heads? Be as wild and creative as you can be; after all, it's a zoo out there.

3. This is a fast-paced play and should be performed at a rapid rate, but slowly enough that all the lines are easily heard. Practice the pace by reading through it once or twice at a ridiculously fast rate, practically speak right over the person before you. Then pull back, but keep the pace fast.

4. If your principal will allow it, write brief advertisements for your performance of this play and read them over the intercom in the morning. Write the ads as though you were the radio characters in the play, such as

   > "This is Mad Mike the Morning Monkey
   > reminding you to attend our play *K-ZOO Radio*,
   > on Friday the 17th. The play will be
   > in Mrs. Andersen's room at 2:30.
   > Be there or be square!"

5. For no good reason except that it's fun, go to the zoo. Go as a field trip, if you can get permission, or meet on a Saturday morning, take lots of pictures, eat a hot dog, and remind yourself of how much fun this used to be when you were a little kid.

In the City Where I Live

Readers

Boy 1		Girl 1
Boy 2		Girl 2
Boy 3		Girl 3
Boy 4	Pets	Girl 4
Boy 5		Girl 5
Boy 6		Girl 6
Boy 7		Girl 7
Boy 8		Girl 8

In the City Where I Live

Notes to the Teacher / Director

Here is a play written in simple language to provide an opportunity for students who need less challenging dialogue: *In The City Where I Live*. As your students flex their reading and acting skills, they share in a lesson about community, loyalty, and working together.

The lines have been divided—Boy 1, Girl 1, Pets—but this is a suggestion only. If you have fewer than eight boys and eight girls, feel free to give one person the lines of, for instance, Boys 1 and 2. And, of course, lines can be distributed to a larger cast by assigning the lines for Boy 1 to two boys—if you like, you can label them in your master script as "Boy 1A" and "Boy 1B." Let the boys and girls portraying the Pets decide whether they would like to read aloud when the script says "All" or whether this little group would rather portray strictly cats and dogs.

Words which may be new to your cast include:
- catalogue
- vacation
- neighbors
- collection
- commit
- restaurants
- grateful

There are opportunities to personalize your play for your own community. Insert the name of your city or town in the first line, then add your high school's team name when that blank space comes along.

Emphasize working together and concentrating when you rehearse the lines that boys and girls say together, such as those marked "All," "All Boys," "All Girls," or "Pets." They should work toward sounding as if their voices have blended together, almost as one voice.

Have fun—invite the community to your performance—and celebrate the city where you live!

(On stage are stools and music stands for your cast. Your students may enter as the play begins, or be "discovered" seated on their stools.)

ALL Welcome to _____ , the city where we live.

GIRL 1 It is our home. Some of us were born here . . .

BOY 1 Some of us moved here . . .

GIRL 1 AND BOY 1 But to all of us . . .

ALL It is home.

BOY 2 We know our neighbors, and we know their pets.

PETS Bark! Bark! Meow!

GIRL 2 AND BOY 3 We look out for each other.

GIRL 2 I have a key to my next-door neighbor's house. When he goes on vacation, I water his plants and feed his pets.

PETS Bark! Bark! Yum!

BOY 4 I look out my window and keep an eye on my neighbor's house. Is that a robber? No—it's just the mailman.

BOY 5 I am the mailman. I bring loved ones' letters . . . and catalogues . . . and bills!

ALL Yuck! Nobody wants bills!

GIRL 3 Nobody wants bills, but we need them. When we pay bills, we pay for things in our city like our trash collection.

BOYS 6, 7, AND 8 We work on the garbage truck in our city. We tell everyone to put their trashcan lids on good and tight—otherwise, their pets make a mess!

PETS Bark! Bark! Sorry!

ALL This is our city. We live here. Our children go to school here.

BOY 1 AND GIRL 4 On the first day of school, we walk with our children to their new classroom.

BOY 2 AND GIRL 5 We meet the new teacher. We see the new desk.

GIRL 6 I am a teacher. I don't like children and I don't work very hard at all. Just kidding!

ALL GIRLS Teachers in our city work hard. They educate our children. See? If not for teachers, we wouldn't know the word "educate."

ALL In the city where we live, parents love their children.

ALL GIRLS They go to watch boys and girls play soccer . . .

BOY 3 "Run, Alice, run! Score the goal!"

ALL BOYS And baseball . . .

GIRL 7 "It's a home run!" they say. "Goodbye, baseball! It's out of the park!"

ALL And when football season rolls around, the whole city turns out to cheer for our team, the _____.

GIRLS 8, 1 AND 2 We all say, "Go, fight, win!"

ALL We cheer for our team because we love our city. We feel pride about where we live.

ALL BOYS And we love that marching band!

GIRL 3 "Band, ten hut!"

ALL In our city, we have firemen and policemen who help to keep us safe.

BOY 4 I am a fireman. I hope our city never has a fire . . . but if one should start, I will be there to put it out.

ONE CAT *(out of PETS)* Meow! Meow!

BOY 4 I'll also get your cat out of a tree.

SAME CAT   Meow! Meow! Thanks!

BOY 4   My friend the policeman drives around town in his patrol car.

BOY 5   I don't want to give you a ticket—so don't drive so fast!

BOY 4   My friend the policeman will catch bad guys and put them in jail.

BOY 5   I DO want to catch bad guys—so don't commit a crime!

ALL   Don't commit a crime in our city. We love it here. We love to be safe.

ALL GIRLS   We have a park where children can play with their friends.

GIRL 4   Mothers take their babies there. They play in the sand.

GIRL 5   Older boys and girls play on the swings.

ALL BOYS   Older boys and girls pretend to be pirates.

BOY 6   They say, "Ahoy mates! Run away before I make you walk the plank!"

ALL GIRLS   In the city where we live, most fathers work at jobs all day. But after work, they can play catch in the park with their sons.

ALL BOYS   In the city where we live, some mothers work at jobs all day, and some mothers stay home with their little children.

ALL GIRLS   We all work hard to have a house . . .

BOY 7   . . . and a car . . .

GIRL 6   . . . and something to eat.

ALL   In the city where we live, mothers and fathers cook good meals for their families.

GIRL 7   But sometimes, families get to go out to eat at restaurants.

ALL BOYS   Sometimes, parents and their children get to have hamburgers, fried chicken, and pizza! *(All BOYS make smacking sounds and lick their lips.)*

ALL GIRLS _____ is a very good restaurant in our town.

They have the best _____ for miles around!

ALL In the city where we live, everyone is grateful for all the blessings there are in a single day.

BOY 8 A nice warm house . . .

GIRL 8 Nice neighbors who care about each other . . .

GIRL 1 Good schools with hard-working teachers . . .

BOY 1 Well-behaved children who do all their chores . . .

GIRL 2 AND BOY 2 Well, ALMOST all their chores . . .

GIRL 3 AND BOY 3 And friendly pets who protect our homes.

PETS Bark! Bark! You're welcome!

BOY 4 This is safety . . .

GIRL 4 This is love . . .

GIRL 5 This is family . . .

BOY 5 This is working together . . .

ALL GIRLS This is . . .

ALL . . . the city where we live.

PETS Bark! Bark! Meow! The end!

Readers' Theatre

48

In the City Where I Live

Follow-up Activities

1. Choose a profession represented in the play. Write a short paper or a short song or a short scene depicting the duties and responsibilities that person has to the community. Consider visiting, calling, or emailing a person who holds that job in your city, and interview him or her about the job. Find out what he or she likes about the job, what the challenges are, and why he or she chose that profession.

2. As a class, discuss what would happen in your city if, for instance, there were no garbage men. Or firemen. Or a police force. What things do we take for granted that would suddenly disappear? How would life change?

3. For two weeks, keep a journal about ways in which you observe members of your community working together. For instance, if your mom agrees to water a neighbor's plants while the neighbor is on vacation, make a note of it. If you see your father helping his brother mend the roof on his garage after a storm, note that. At the end of the two weeks, share with the class your findings. Does your community work together to help each other? If you don't see very many examples of that kind of cooperation, how could it improve?

4. In recent years, terrible hurricanes have hit the Gulf Coast of America, forcing many people out of their homes. Discuss the ways in which Americans have worked together to take care of these displaced people. Do you think your family would open its home to a family which had lost theirs? If so, what good things could happen? What things could result which would not be so good? If you know someone who was affected by these natural disasters, share his or her story with the class.

Big Game, Little Guy

Readers

Willie	Coach Ball	Trey Aikin
Catherine	Football Team Members	Dave
Dad	Snarl	A Scot
Granddad	Slammer	Another Scot
Mom	Cheerleaders	Quarterback (QB)
Crunch		Ms. Fajardo

Big Game, Little Guy

Notes to the Teacher / Director:

Go! Fight! Swim? Swim, indeed, if your team is called the Salmon and you go to Central High School. In this readers' theatre offering, the cast of which can expand to include a large number of young actors, it's football season and time for "the big game." Our hero, Willie Oliver, has wanted to play football since he was really small—and that's the problem; he's still really small. He lives in a little town, however, and so he's allowed to sign up for sports. Coach Ball hints that his chances of making the team will be increased if he tutors Crunch Alderson, football star and not-so-good-in-English student. Willie's mom is an English teacher, and Willie who's been diagramming sentences since he could walk, agrees to help.

The week of the big game with rival Highland Park High School arrives, and Crunch gets bad news; even though he and Willie have been working hard, he's failing English by two points. Willie urges Crunch to speak to his reasonable English teacher about extra credit. As Crunch runs off to Ms. Fajardo's room, Willie heads for the locker room to suit up for the game. Crunch's back-up player is injured and must leave the game, but Crunch has managed to be reinstated on the team. He has been allowed to retake the test, this time remembering his lessons by way of the grammatical desserts Willie's mom has baked for him. Just when everything seems to be going the way of the Central High Salmon, Crunch gets injured as well! Willie Oliver is the only boy left to fill the spot. His small size and speed work for him; he is able to elude the Scots defenders and runs the ball in for the winning score. All agree that Willie saved the day twice—once by helping Crunch learn his English, and once by scoring the final TD.

There is a chorus of cheerleaders who punctuate the gridiron action with cheers, some recognizable, some new and improved. There is also a scene in the locker room in which several football players speak together. You can use both of these groups to include as many students as you like. If your group is small, let Catherine say all the cheers, and let Crunch, Slammer, and Snarl do the team parts.

There are several opportunities for interesting characters to emerge within this play. Certainly Crunch can be a stereotypical, oafish football player; Catherine can be the cheerleader everybody remembers (or was!); and the sports announcers can be patterned after any number of on-air folk. Likewise, the growling Coach Ball, the sweet and sassy Mom, the elderly Granddad, and so on. . . There are plenty of times when young voices can create believable characterizations.

The humor is broad, but the lessons are good ones: It's not enough to be tough on the field; you've got to keep your academics up to par as well. There is also an underlying theme of teamwork. Crunch, Willie, and the rest of the team realize that they must work together—in more ways than one—to be successful in life and on the football field.

The following words may be new to your students:

• conjugate	• demonstrating	• scrimmage	• ineligible	• nominative
• optimistic	• declaratory	• preposition	• emblem	• objective
• participle	• crucial	• concussions	• academic	

(Place script notebooks on music stands, and arrange chairs and music stands as you like; WIILLIE should probably be in the center. You may wish to have the CHEERLEADERS together at one side of the acting area.)

WILLIE   Hello, everyone, and thank you for coming! My name is Willie Oliver . . . *(a pause; then, to audience:)* . . . er . . . that's your cue. You're supposed to say "Hi Willie." Let's try it again. My name is Willie . . . *(looks expectantly at the audience as they, hopefully, reply)*. That was great. You are an audience that really knows how to take directions.

CATHERINE   Willie—can we get on with it? These people have lives!

WILLIE   Sorry, Catherine. *(to audience)* That's Catherine. She's the head cheerleader for the Mighty Fighting Salmon of Central High School.

CATHERINE   Go, fight, swim!

WILLIE   Catherine . . . and I . . . and all these other people . . . *(rest of the cast waves)* . . . are here to tell you the story of the big game that almost wasn't. I mean, it was always "big" but it was almost . . . well, wait, I don't want to give anything away . . .

CATHERINE   Willie, for Pete's sake! These people will have grandchildren before you get this story told!

WILLIE   Some of them already have grandchildren.

CATHERINE   I mean the kids!

WILLIE   OK, let me start at the very beginning . . .

CATHERINE   Willie . . .

WILLIE   OK, not the very beginning. How about right here: I love football. Before I started to school, I used to sit with my dad and grandfather and watch the Dallas Cowboys *(or insert local pro team here)*. They used to say to me:

DAD   Son—someday that will be you! When you grow up, you can play football just like those guys!

GRANDDAD   That's right, Willie! When you get to be just a little bit bigger, you can pass and catch and kick like the rest of them.

WILLIE   "Ya mean it?" I would say. "I can really play football?"

DAD   You bet!

WILLIE   . . . Dad would answer.

DAD & GRANDDAD   Just as soon as you grow to be a little bit taller.

Readers' Theatre

WILLIE But that was the problem. My dad was tall—but I didn't take after him. I took after my tiny . . . little . . . mom.

MOM Good things come in small packages!

WILLIE By the way—I know what you're all thinking. My name is Willie—and I'm short. So go ahead—say it. Say, "Wee Willie Winkie." Let's get it over with. Everybody now:

(A pause as the audience says "Wee Willie Winkie.")

Thank you. I'm glad we've gotten that out of our systems. Anyway, my dad and my grandfather kept encouraging me.

DAD Don't worry, Son . . . you're sure to grow taller!

GRANDDAD I bet you're six feet tall by the time you start high school!

MOM I think you're perfect just like you are. Who needs football! Let's conjugate a verb.

WILLIE I forgot to tell you . . . my mother is a tiny, little . . . English teacher.

MOM "The cat licked its paws." Come on, Willie, quick! Apostrophe or no?

WILLIE No apostrophe, Mom. Possessive form of "it" is "its" with no apostrophe.

MOM Perfect! You're my little grammar guy!

WILLIE I was happy to be Mom's little grammar guy—but I also wanted to be the Salmon's big, strong, tough football-playing guy!

CATHERINE If wishes were horses, we would all ride.

WILLIE Time passed. I had my eleventh birthday . . .

DAD I bet you go shooting up with you turn twelve! Yes sir, when you're celebrating your twelfth birthday, I bet you're pushing six feet.

WILLIE And I had my twelfth birthday . . .

GRANDDAD Thirteen! That's the age. When you become a teenager, I bet you become tall as . . . as tall as . . . someone really tall.

WILLIE When I turned 13, the men in my family seemed to give up.

DAD There's nothing wrong with playing soccer, Willie, my boy.

GRANDDAD Or being a jockey!

WILLIE Yikes. Soccer? A jockey?! I wanted to play football, and that was that.

CATHERINE	Lucky for you, Central High School is the size of a postage stamp.
WILLIE	Our school isn't very big. Which means that if there's nothing else you need to take first period—you can sign up for football. Which I did. Dad and Granddad were overjoyed.
DAD	Terrific, Son! Let's go out into the yard and toss the ball around!
GRANDDAD	You two go ahead. I'm going to put a first-aid kit together.
WILLIE	Granddad wasn't too optimistic.
MOM	Wait, Willie! "We went to the store and shopped all day." Comma after "store"?
WILLIE	No, Mom. One subject, two verbs. No comma.
MOM	Nothing beats a good grammar lesson on a fall afternoon!
WILLIE	Right, Mom . . .
DAD	Willie, come on! Let's play some football in the present tense!
WILLIE	Gotta go, Mom! Later!
MOM	"The team is . . . or the team are . . . ?"
WILLIE	The team is. Now let me go see if I can make the team!
CATHERINE	*(impatiently, hurrying him along)* So your Dad worked with you every day after school . . .
WILLIE	Yes, and on the first day of practice, I walked into the locker room, trying to look as tall as I possibly could . . .
CRUNCH	Hey—who's the little guy?
WILLIE	*(to audience)* That's Crunch. Crunch Alderson. I've heard that he lifts guys like me . . .
CRUNCH	I lift guys like you instead of barbells!
WILLIE	See what I mean?
CRUNCH	What are you doing in the field house? We're about to go work out, not lift weights!
WILLIE	*(to CRUNCH)* Hey, Crunch. *(to audience)* I said boldly. *(back to CRUNCH)* I'm here to work out. I'm on the team . . . that is, I'm taking football this year.

Readers' Theatre

CRUNCH What? You're taking football? You mean you're going to be our water boy, don't you?

WILLIE No, Crunch. I mean I'm going to take sports this period and play for the mighty fighting Salmon.

CATHERINE Yayyy, Salmon!

WILLIE Catherine, you weren't there!

CATHERINE I know. I'm just full of pep and school spirit.

CRUNCH The day a little guy like you makes the team is the day I . . . well, no, I was going to say I would quit, but that wouldn't be true. I want to play, no matter what . . . I know. The day a little guy like you makes the team is the day that I say "What?
A little guy like that made the team?"

(CRUNCH smiles as if he has just come up with a brilliant statement.)

WILLIE That's our Crunch.

CRUNCH Just don't get in my way, squirt.

WILLIE I was about to assure him that I would try very hard to stay out of his way, when Coach Ball entered. By the way . . . have you ever noticed about peoples' names? Like, Coach Ball. I mean, he's the football coach, and his name is "Ball." I have a dentist whose name is "Dr. Filler." And the guy who works at the hamburger place is "Mr. Ketchup With Your Fries." Not really. I made that one up.

COACH BALL All right, all you Salmon, listen up! This is the year that we're going to be state champions. Do you hear me? We're not going to be district champs, or champs of the area, or champs of the neighborhood. We're going to state and we're going to win when we get there! Any questions?

CRUNCH Yeah, Coach. If we're going to win state, why do we have to play all the games that come before it? Why can't they just send us the trophy, like in the mail or something?

COACH BALL Crunch . . . go tape up your knees.

CRUNCH Why? I haven't even injured them yet.

COACH BALL *(ignoring him)* And not only that . . . before we even get to state . . . this is the year . . . we're going to beat . . . say it with me . . .

**FOOTBALL
TEAM MEMBERS** HIGHLAND PARK!

Readers' Theatre

56

COACH BALL	That's right! This year they're going down! I'm tired of those sissy, kilt-wearing Scots beating us every year!
SNARL	The Coach is right! We can take them this year!
COACH BALL	Thank you, Snarl. I'm so glad that someone named "Snarl" has told me that I'm right.
SNARL	No problem, Coach. We've got your back.
SLAMMER	I've heard that they've got a lot of returning starters. It may be tougher than we think!
COACH BALL	Don't start with me, Slammer! They may have a lot of returning starters, but guess what we have?
FOOTBALL TEAM MEMBERS	The . . .
COACH BALL	Yes, yes!
FOOTBALL TEAM MEMBERS	Passion . . .
COACH BALL	Passion, yes, the passion to do what?
FOOTBALL TEAM MEMBERS	THE PASSION TO KILL!!!
COACH BALL	That's right! The passion to kill! And what do they have?
CRUNCH	The passion to "kilt"?
COACH BALL	No, Crunch, they've got nothing! We're going to pound Highland Park into the ground and step on them as we go to state. Any questions?
ALL FOOTBALL TEAM MEMBERS	No, Coach!
COACH BALL	Then what are you waiting for? Get on out to that field and practice, practice, practice! *(claps his hands)* Everybody out! Get going! Remember: the passion to kill!
FOOTBALL TEAM MEMBERS	Right!
COACH BALL	Go! Fight! Win! Now, before you run out of here making noise, here are this year's varsity cheerleaders to inspire you. Girls?
CATHERINE	Ready, OK!

CHEERLEADERS	Who cares who's on your team,
	The Salmon's gonna swim upstream.
	We will charge, and we will fight!
	We will win this game tonight!
	The coach's son is quarterback,
	He will lead a sneak attack.
	The other team will run like snails
	The Salmon's gonna tip the scales!

(Ad libbing cheers)

All right! Go Salmon! Go! Fight! Swim!

COACH BALL Now scram! Go hurt each other! Say, Crunch? Stay behind, will you, son? And you, too, Willie.

WILLIE *(To audience)* Now I have to tell you that my heart pounded when the coach asked me to stay behind. What was he going to do? Kick me out? Tell me I must have wandered into the field house by mistake? Torture me for Crunch's entertainment? But no! He said . . .

COACH BALL I want to welcome you, Willie, personally, to the sports program here at Central.

WILLIE Thanks, Coach!

COACH BALL You know that, as a team, we will always get more done and be more successful if we work together to achieve our goals. We're better than the parts of our sums. I mean . . . we add up to something better than . . . aw heck, you know what I mean.

WILLIE I can honestly say I have no idea.

CRUNCH Willie, you goober! You said "idea." It's supposed to be "ideal." Like "I have a good ideal!" I bet you're really flustrated in English class!!!

COACH BALL It's like this, son. Crunch here is a great running back. He's fast and he's strong and he's big. But . . . er, Crunch, would you do me a favor? Go over to the equipment locker and see if it's locked. If it is, come back and get the key.

CRUNCH You've got it, Coach.

COACH BALL The thing is, Willie—he's not very good in English class.

WILLIE What shocking news!

COACH BALL It is hard to imagine; I mean, he seems so bright and all.

WILLIE *(aside, to audience)* About as bright as a really dirty light bulb! With dead bugs all over it and dirt and mud and gross . . .

COACH BALL	Willie? You still with me?
WILLIE	Yes, Coach. Sorry.
COACH BALL	As you know, in our state, students have to be passing their academic subjects in order to play football and other sports. Toward the end of last season, Crunch was ineligible because he failed English.
WILLIE	So what does this have to do with me?
COACH BALL	I know how much you want to play football—your dad and I have been friends for years. And I want to work with you as much as I can to give you your best shot at getting to play. In return . . . sort of . . . I'd like you to work with Crunch and make sure he passes English.
WILLIE	What! You want me to help him in English?
COACH BALL	If it wouldn't be too much trouble. I mean, I know you're going to be busy, with football practice and all . . .
WILLIE	*(to audience)* Now he was really fighting dirty. Making me imagine myself at football practice, sweating, drinking Gatorade or water out of a jug with the school emblem on it. Getting one of the student trainers to get me a cold towel . . .
COACH BALL	Willie? I feel like I keep losing you.
WILLIE	No, I'm here. And, of course, I'll be willing to work with Crunch. Just tell him to call me or meet me at my locker after school when he needs help. Or maybe he can come over to my house. My mom teaches English, you know.
COACH BALL	Oh yes, that's right! That had completely slipped my mind!
WILLIE	*(aside, to audience)* Yeah, right. *(to COACH BALL)* I'll be glad to do whatever I can for the good of the Salmon.
COACH BALL	There's the boy. Now, go . . .
CRUNCH	*(interrupting)* OK, Coach, I went to the equipment locker, and it wasn't locked. But I forgot whether I was supposed to come back and get the key if it was locked or if it was unlocked.
COACH BALL	You did fine, Crunch. Now please walk Willie out to the practice field, won't you?
CRUNCH	I gotta walk Short Stuff out? Come on, Coach! He knows the way!
COACH BALL	Maybe—but if you'll walk together you'll get there faster!
WILLIE	*(aside, to audience)* When he said that, he actually looked at me and winked!

(COACH BALL looks at audience and winks, demonstrating.)

 Readers' Theatre

See?! Just like that. Like we had this great secret between us, and he was going to make the world safe for football. But—I wanted to play—so what could I do but agree to help Crunch pass English.

CHEERLEADERS Push 'em back, push 'em back, way back!

WILLIE Football season started.

CHEERLEADERS Crunch, Crunch, he's our man!
If he can't crunch 'em, no one can!

WILLIE First we played the Wildcats from West High School . . .

CHEERLEADERS N-O-T-H-I-N-G,
That's what Wildcats mean to me!
Nothing! Absolutely nothing!
(Ad lib cheers)
All right! Y'all yell! Go Salmon!

WILLIE I sat on the bench. Crunch caught a pass in the end zone and won the game with three seconds left on the scoreboard.

CHEERLEADERS Y'all are hitting, but we aren't bruisin'!
Look on the scoreboard and see who's losin'!
(Ad lib cheers)
All right! Y'all yell! Go Salmon!

WILLIE Monday after football practice, Crunch came over, and we worked on prepositional phrases. My mother made cookies with icing that spelled prepositions.

MOM Here, Crunch! Have a cookie with "about" on it!

CRUNCH Thank you, ma'am! I love cookies with "about" on them. In fact, I love "about" any cookie there is! Get it? *(laughs in a "hyuck hyuck" manner)*

MOM I do get it! And now where's that cookie?

CRUNCH What do you mean? Wasn't I supposed to eat it?

WILLIE Yes, you were supposed to eat it, Crunch. And, since you ate it, where is it now?

CRUNCH It's . . . not on the plate! "Not" must be the preposition thingy. Or maybe plate?

WILLIE & MOM *(sighing)* It's gonna be a long season.

WILLIE The next week, as some of us were wrapping sprained wrists, and some of us were wishing we had a pillow to make the bench softer, we played the Vikings from North High School.

CHEERLEADERS Hello, hello? Our phones are ringing!

We think we hear the fat lady singing!
(Ad lib cheers)
All right! Y'all yell! Go Salmon!

WILLIE   It was rainy and the ball was slippery. The quarterback passed to Snarl, but Snarl was being covered. So Crunch ran from the other side of the field and caught the pass intended for Snarl and ran it in for the big TD. The bench was a little slippery, too. Once I almost slipped right off and landed in a puddle.

CHEERLEADERS   Rain is falling and it's wet!
Will we beat y'all? Yes—you bet!

WILLIE   A few games went by . . .

CHEERLEADERS   Go, Salmon! Beat the Eagles!

WILLIE   Crunch kept coming over for help, and he did OK in English, but not great.

CHEERLEADERS   Fight, Salmon, fight! Win this game tonight!

WILLIE   I continued to practice with the team, and I was pretty good! I don't want to brag, but I was . . . fast. Little—but fast.

CATHERINE   What do you mean, you don't want to brag? What's "I was fast."?

WILLIE   It's a statement of fact, Catherine. A declaratory sentence. A sentence used to make a statement.

CATHERINE   Whatever!

WILLIE   Finally, it was the week of the big game. Highland Park. Our enemy. And, worse—it was our homecoming. They especially like to beat us in our home stadium. We had had a good season, but we'd lost one game. We were beaten by Our Lady of the Pigskin Catholic School. They beat us soundly and made the cheerleaders furious by making a big butcher paper sign that said, "We always eat fish on Fridays."

CATHERINE   That was just cruel.

WILLIE   Highland Park was undefeated. And Crunch was failing English. I don't know how it happened. We worked together almost every week—and he had failed a couple of tests, but I didn't think his average was that bad. But sure enough, he came over to my house on Monday of the Highland Park game with his progress report. Not much progress had been made.

COACH BALL   Willie, I need to talk to you, son.

WILLIE   Coach Ball called me into his office after practice.

COACH BALL   Crunch is failing English.

WILLIE   Yes sir. I know. But I don't know how . . .

COACH BALL   *(interrupting)* He's crucial to our running game, Willie. We've just got to have him in the game against HP.

WILLIE   I think he has a test . . .

COACH BALL   *(interrupting)* Now, son, I'm counting on you. We need him passing that course by Friday night's game.

WILLIE   He's supposed to come over on . . .

COACH BALL   *(interrupting)* Good, good, that sounds great. Now go out there and give it the old Salmon . . . the old Salmon study . . . study session . . . you know what I mean, son.

WILLIE   Coach, I don't know what more I can . . .

COACH BALL   *(interrupting)* Good, son, good. I knew you would understand. Now go home and get some rest . . . or study with Crunch . . . and let's beat Highland Park! Go! Fight! Win!

WILLIE   When I got to my house, Crunch was already there. This time he had brought his buddies, Slammer and Snarl. I don't know why, except maybe for moral support. Also, my mother was hemming Catherine's homecoming dress, so she was there, too. It was hard to concentrate.

CATHERINE   Oh my gosh, Willie's mom, this is so awesome of you to hem my dress! My mother does not know how to sew, and I don't want to trip on it when I walk out on the field with my dad . . . to see if I . . . *(starts to sniffle)* . . . was lucky enough . . . *(sniffling)* . . . to be named Homecoming Queen for Central High School! This is the moment I've been waiting for my whole life!

MOM   "For which I've been waiting," dear.

CATHERINE   You've been waiting your whole life, too? That's a long wait, Willie's mom!

MOM   No, I mean you should say . . .

WILLIE   Mom . . . pick your battles.

MOM   Right dear.

WILLIE   So, Crunch . . .

CRUNCH   Willie. I'm not passing English.

WILLIE   I heard.

CRUNCH   You gotta help me, man! The team won't have the passion to kill without me!

SNARL Dude, we always have the passion to kill. We just can't always do the killing part.

SLAMMER We sure won't get any killing done if you're not in the game, Crunch! Come on! Get to studying! Don't mind us; we're just over here eating.

MOM I think Crunch is wrestling with nominative and objective pronouns, dear. So I baked some "who / whom" brownies!

CRUNCH This rocks, Willie. If I get it right, I get a brownie! It's awesome!

WILLIE Mom's brownies are awesome even if she doesn't have pronouns on top. OK, Crunch, let's see the study sheet for the test. And Slammer and Snarl . . . don't eat all the study aids.

SLAMMER & SNARL *(with mouths full)* We won't eat any more, dude!

WILLIE OK, Crunch. Is this right: "Who is on the phone?"

CRUNCH Yes. I mean—wait. "Whom" always sounds smarter than "Who." No—I'll say "Whom is on the phone."

SLAMMER The Who! Dude! That was an awesome band from like the '60s or '70s . . . or maybe it was the '80s, I can't remember.

SNARL They rocked! Crunch, dude, the answer must be "Who" because of "The Who."

CRUNCH Would that be funny, dude, if they had named their band "The Whom"? That would totally rock!

CATHERINE Willie's mom! This looks wonderful! I mean . . . oh wait, I want to get this right . . . it looks wonderfully. Longer word, better word. Right Willie?

WILLIE *(aside, to audience)* It's going to be a long season. Anyway, we worked long and hard that night on nominative and objective case pronouns. I would tell you some examples of our work, but you might think I was trying to trick you into learning something. Let me just say that we worked through dinner—Mom baked some "she and her" muffins and a "they and them" pie. We worked while we ate and then worked some more. We worked hard every night. Thursday was Crunch's English test. On Friday . . .

CRUNCH Dude! Mrs. Fajardo has posted the English test grades!

WILLIE . . . Crunch called out to me in the hall.

CRUNCH Let's go see how I did!

WILLIE We ran through the crowds like we had tacklers on our heels. We faked left, right, up the middle. We raced up to Mrs. Fajardo's classroom door and . . .

CRUNCH   I failed.

WILLIE   You made a 68.
(to audience) A 70 is considered passing in our school.
(to CRUNCH) You made a 68.

CRUNCH   Oh, no! What am I going to do! The game's tonight!

WILLIE   Here's what you're going to do. Go to Mrs. Fajardo and see if there's anything you can do for extra credit. I would go with you, but I've got to get over to the field house.

CRUNCH   You're going to the field house without me!

WILLIE   Yes I am, but you go see Mrs. Fajardo. She's a fair teacher! See what you can do! If she cuts you any slack, I'll see you on the sidelines. I'll be the one with the clean uniform, sitting on the bench.

CRUNCH   OK, Willie. Wish me luck. And Willie . . . thanks for all the help.

WILLIE   Crunch, you're welcome, but it's up to you now. Go see your teacher!

DAVE   Welcome, everyone, to Upstream Stadium, home of the Salmon of Central High School! I'll be your announcer for the evening; my name is Dave. Here with me is one of the all-time great quarterbacks of Central High, class of *(insert a year that was several years ago)*. Trey Aikin.

TREY AIKIN   Hey, Dave, how's it goin'?

DAVE   Great, Trey, just great. Say—I bet you were "achin'" a few times when you left this stadium!

TREY AIKIN   What do you mean, Dave?

DAVE   It was a little joke, Trey; your name sounds like . . . oh never mind. Today's contest will surely be an exciting one! The Salmon of Central High versus the Scots of Highland Park! This rivalry goes back many years, Trey; do you have any idea how it got started?

TREY AIKIN   Well, Dave, I believe it got started when both teams really wanted to win the game real bad.

DAVE   Er . . . yes, I guess that was it! OK! Well, Central's marching band, The Sounds of Salmon, is climbing into the stands. They certainly sound great this year! And three girl drum majors! Aren't they cute!

TREY AIKIN   Look, Dave! Some guys wearing skirts! That looks weird!

DAVE   I'd forgotten how many concussions you sustained while you were playing football, Trey. But that's absolutely right, those guys do appear to be wearing skirts! They're kilts, however, and that's the Fighting Scotsmen Band from Highland Park High! They've chosen to wear the traditional Scottish kilts as part of their marching uniform.

TREY AIKIN They don't look very kilt to me! They look alive and well!

DAVE Uh . . . yes, Trey, I guess they do look alive. OK, the teams are taking the field now—we'll be singing the national anthem soon—uh oh! What's this! I see the Salmon football team, and there's no Crunch Alderson!

TREY AIKIN He plays football really good.

DAVE Yes, he does . . . but . . . what's this? Somebody has handed me a note . . . he's ineligible! He must have failed a course, but he's not on the sidelines with the rest of the team! Oh no, this is not good for the Salmon of Central High!

TREY AIKIN No, it's not, Dave! Uh . . . why isn't it good for the team again? I forgot.

DAVE Never mind, Trey, never mind. Gee, folks, Coach Ball seems really upset! He seems to be talking to . . . who is that? Who's that little guy? I don't remember seeing him before. Let me look at the roster . . . Oliver? Yes, Willie Oliver. Wonder what they're discussing.

COACH BALL Willie, where is he? I need Crunch in this starting line-up!

WILLIE He's talking to his English teacher, Coach. Maybe she'll see reason!

COACH BALL Well, you know, Willie, you did your best. I know you must have shared your home with Crunch and used your valuable time to help him. I know he's doing a lot better, but he must've fallen a little bit short.

WILLIE Gee, wouldn't it have been nice if that's what he really said? Sorry to trick you . . . what he actually said was:

COACH BALL I BETTER SEE CRUNCH ALDERSON SUITED UP BEFORE THE END OF THE FIRST QUARTER OR I'M GOING TO GRIND YOU AND YOUR ENGLISH BOOK UP INTO A FINE POWDER AND DUST THE FIELD WITH YOU! DO YOU UNDERSTAND ME, OLIVER?

WILLIE And believe me, he said it in capital letters. See? *(holds up script for the audience to see)* All caps.

CHEERLEADERS Bacon, toast, ham and eggs
HP Scots have hairy legs!
Go, Salmon!

WILLIE The game started. All things considered, it was pretty close.

DAVE You know, Trey, seeing as how this is a Crunch-less game, the Salmon are holding their own pretty well. Of course, there was that intercepted pass that the Scots ran back for a TD . . .

TREY Yeah, that was tough to watch. I mean, I could see it OK, I just didn't want to.

DAVE Check. And the guy who's playing in Crunch's position isn't doing too bad . . . oh wait! I spoke too soon! He's down . . . the trainers are coming onto the field! Looks like he may be injured.

WILLIE The Scots were playing dirty. They were hitting late and holding and grabbing facemasks, but all just out of the referees' sight. Crunch's replacement was just getting up and being led off the field . . .

DAVE He just looks like he's shaken up a bit, Trey. He's walking on his own steam . . . wait a minute! What's this? Is that Crunch Alderson I see running toward Coach Ball?

TREY I guess so, Dave! He's wearing a uniform that says "Alderson" on the back, and unless he broke into Crunch's locker, that's him!

CHEERLEADERS We love fish that swim upstream!
We hate Scots; they're really mean!
Go, Salmon, go!

WILLIE Out of the corner of my eye, I saw Crunch running up. And he was indeed wearing his uniform!

CRUNCH Willie! I'm in! Mrs. Fajardo gave me the extra two points!

WILLIE How, Crunch? What happened?

CRUNCH No time to explain now! Coach Ball—can I go in?

COACH BALL Yes, Crunch, yes! Get in there and turn this thing around! Oliver—good work. The Salmon owe you!

WILLIE It was nothing, Coach. Now can I . . .

COACH BALL *(ignoring him)* All right, team, Crunch is back! Now, let's put some points on the scoreboard!

WILLIE The game went on . . .

DAVE What a game! It's almost the half, and the score is tied. Crunch Alderson's 50-yard run was a thing of beauty. He had defenders hanging on him like . . .

TREY Like ornaments on a Christmas tree!

DAVE	Yes, just like that.
WILLIE	It was an amazing game. They'd score, we'd score. They'd kick a field goal, we'd score. They'd kick a field goal. It went like that—back and forth, back and forth—until the fourth quarter. We were three points behind. The quarterback went back to pass . . .
DAVE	The QB is back to pass—he looks—he seems to be trying to find Crunch Alderson—there he is . . . oh oh! What's this!
WILLIE	A big, ugly defensive tackle for the Scots broke through the line and hit Crunch right in the knees. Crunch went down—and he stayed down.
TREY	Looks like Crunch got crunched, Dave!
DAVE	Yes, Trey, it does. The trainers are running out . . . his parents are joining him on the field . . . the players are taking the knee.
WILLIE	Crunch had been hit by a six-foot-four defensive player for Highland Park. I don't want to give you the idea that he was too old to be playing, but I saw him get into a car later that had a bumper sticker that said "Ask me about my grandkids." But, no matter how old the guy was, Crunch was down.
DAVE	Oh, this could be the game for the Salmon, Trey. Crunch's second-string player was hurt earlier—now Crunch—who else do they have?
COACH BALL	Willie! Willie Oliver! Get over here!
WILLIE	I looked left and right. He couldn't have been talking to me!
COACH BALL	Yes, you, grammar man. You're going in for Crunch! Look lively!
WILLIE	I couldn't believe it! I was finally getting to play!
COACH BALL	I know you probably can't believe you're finally getting to play . . . but, well, I don't have anybody else. Get out there and . . . try to stay alive.
CHEERLEADERS	Come on Salmon, don't be sad! We love you, and we hate plaid! Go, Salmon!
WILLIE	What happened next seems so weird and unreal that I almost can't believe it myself.
CATHERINE	I'm a witness, though! I was on top of the cheerleader pyramid—I could see for miles and miles.
WILLIE	The Scots were saying mean things to me under their breath . . .

A SCOT	Where's your teddy bear, little man?
ANOTHER SCOT	Isn't it past your bedtime, little dude? Somebody read him *Goodnight Moon* before he starts to cry!
WILLIE	It was pretty awful, and I know I should've been scared to death but I was just so amazed to be in the game! I was so amazed that I didn't pay attention and . . . ooof!
TREY & DAVE	Ouch!
DAVE	That's got to hurt! What was Central's QB thinking, tossing the ball to that little guy! Of course he was tackled before he even touched the laces!
DAD	That's OK, Son! Get up and try it again!
GRANDDAD	We're pulling for you, boy! Go! Fight! Win!
MOM	That's right, sweetie! It's you for whom we're yelling! I mean . . . we're yelling for . . . oh heck, go Willie go!
WILLIE	I'd been tackled behind the line of scrimmage. I saw stars.
DAVE	I bet he's seeing stars right about now!
TREY	You mean like movie stars?
DAVE	No, Trey, I mean he's had the stuffing knocked out of him! And look at that! Unbelievably, the QB is going to hit him again!
WILLIE	In the huddle, our quarterback told me that he was going to toss it to me once more.
QB	They'll never see it coming!
WILLIE	. . . he said.
QB	Maybe you'll break loose.
WILLIE	Or maybe I'll just break, I thought to myself. But, of course, I lined up with the rest of the team—the QB called . . .
QB	Hut! Hut!
DAVE	He's back to pass . . . he's looking . . . could it be? He's looking for Oliver again!
TREY	Looka there, Dave! He caught it!
DAVE	It's Willie Oliver on the carry . . . he's to the 55, the 50-yard line—he's in Scots territory now . . . and he's still going! Look at him race!
DAD	Go, Willie, go!
GRANDDAD	The boy's got wheels! Look at him tearing up the turf!

DAVE   He's on the 40, the 35 . . . the crowd is going wild!

CAST   *(Everybody who's not speaking starts to cheer softly, as if in the background.)*

CHEERLEADERS   You might think this cheer is silly
But we would like to say GO WILLIE!
So we will.
GO, WILLIE!

TREY   I think he's going to do it! I think he's going all the way!

DAVE   It looks that way, Trey! Holy smokes—he's running through defenders;
they're tripping all over each other trying to catch him!

DAD   That's the way, Son! Go for the big TD!

DAVE   Ladies and gentlemen, this crowd is going wild! He's at the 10, the 5 . . .
TOUCHDOWN Central High Salmon! Wee Willie Winkie ran through the town
and across the goal line—the Salmon lead by six points!

ALL   *(cheer and whistle)*

WILLIE   No, it wasn't a dream, and I'm not going to say "April Fools" or anything.
The Scots were so surprised that I was even in the game, and that I was about
to carry the ball for the second time—I was wide open. And, as previously
boasted, I am fast.

CATHERINE   You boast all you want to, Willie Boy! You pulled the Salmon ahead, and then
Bryce kicked the extra point in the last seconds of the game. I screamed so hard
I pulled a throat muscle and had to wear a turtleneck to school the next day!

WILLIE   Thanks, Catherine. And congratulations on getting Homecoming Queen.

CATHERINE   Thank you, Willie. It was . . . my life's dream . . . *(starts to cry)*

DAVE   And the Salmon of Central High beat the Highland Park Scots 42–38, thanks to an
amazing run by Willie Oliver!

Willie   When I finally caught my breath, the rest of the team was there, lifting me up onto
their shoulders and singing . . . well, they were trying to sing "For He's a Jolly
Good Fellow" but they didn't know that song, so they sang "We Will Rock You."
It was just as good.

When I finally got over to Crunch, I found out that when he got to Mrs. Fajardo's
room, he remembered all the food my mother had made him, and he named all of
it to Mrs. Fajardo. He told her about the preposition cookies and the who/whom
brownies—it seems he was able to remember the English lessons when he thought
about the desserts.

Readers' Theatre

CRUNCH Mrs. Fajardo was so impressed, she said I could take the test over again. I did—and this time I remembered—and I passed—and I offered to get Willie's mom to make her some of the cookies and stuff. She said . . .

MRS. FAJARDO Throw in some brownies, and you've got yourself a deal.

CRUNCH So I was back on the passing side of the grade book, and back to receiving passes in the game.

MOM It will be my pleasure to bake for Crunch's English teacher! Maybe she'd like to come over and visit some time—I have a hankering to diagram a sentence!

WILLIE In the end, though, Crunch had to pass that English test—and he did. Oh, and he was OK from his injury. It was his knee, and it was pretty twisted—but it was all right in a couple of weeks. The most amazing thing of all was that Coach Ball said to me . . .

COACH BALL Son, you really came through for us. You saved the day twice. One, getting Crunch through that little English problem he had, and putting him back in the game. And two—the game-winning TD. Crunch will need to stay off of that knee for a while, and as far as I'm concerned, you're starting next week. Welcome to the team, son! You do have the passion to kill!

DAD I knew he could do it!

MOM We're all proud of you, Willie!

GRANDDAD Well, what're we waiting for? Let's go celebrate!

CRUNCH I think you mean, "For what are we waiting," don't you, Willie's Granddad?

GRANDDAD I guess I do at that, Crunch. I guess I do at that.

WILLIE OK, that's the story. I never gave up my dream and I helped Crunch to keep his dream alive. He's learned that slamming people to the ground isn't enough—you've got to slam those academics to the ground as well. I guess all that's left is to cheer . . .

CAST Thank you so much, that's our play!
We're glad you could be here today!
Work hard, play hard, keep it real
And always keep the passion to kill!

(waving and ad libbing)

GOODBYE, EVERYBODY!
THANKS FOR COMING!

Big Game, Little Guy

Follow-up Activities

1. In the play, Willie helps Crunch study English. When Crunch fails the test, Willie gives him some ideas of how to bring up his grade. What if Willie and Crunch would have figured out a way for Willie to give Crunch the answers? Crunch would have passed and gotten to play—but why wouldn't that have been a good solution? How would that have hurt Crunch rather than help him? Discuss your answers with the class.

2. Which gets the most attention and emphasis in your school, academics or sports? Write a short paper expressing your opinion about whether this is good or not. Support your opinion with ideas about how sports prepare students for life as adults. What about academic studies?

3. Make "spirit posters" and decorate your room before your performance. Get crepe paper streamers in your school colors and hang them from the ceiling. Or, decide what color the Salmon of Central High should be. (How about . . . salmon?) Decorate the room with streamers and balloons in that color. Give a prize to the poster your teacher chooses to be the most spirited.

4. Divide into groups of two. Choose one of the following scenes, write it, and read it to the class. (Play the parts as you wish; you don't have to play the part that is yours in the actual cast.)
   - Coach Ball and Crunch running into each other at a movie
   - Mom and Dad shopping for groceries a few minutes before the Dallas Cowboys are about to play on television
   - Granddad and Catherine talking about fashion
   - Willie and Slammer talking about what they want to do when they grow up
   - Trey Aikin and Crunch discussing current events
   - Dave the sports announcer and Snarl doing a commercial for dishwashing liquid
   - Two Highland Park Scots looking ahead to the future
   - Mrs. Fajardo telling her husband about her day at school

   Feel free to make up your own unlikely (and probably humorous) situations for two of the characters from the play. What would they say? How comfortable or uncomfortable would they be? How would the audience be able to tell how they feel?

Readers' Theatre

At The Fence

Readers

Alex

Cindy

Mattie

At The Fence

Notes to the Teacher / Director:

At the Fence is a play about two girls who meet at the common fence between their properties, and continue to meet there at important times in their lives. It deals with the friendships that can develop over the years, and how helpful it can be to "have yourself a friend," regardless of where you meet.

This play will be an excellent vehicle to showcase two girls with lots of expression in their voices and in their faces. There is a male part which also presents an opportunity for expression and conveying emotion. This role, Alex, is Mattie's father who has recently lost his wife and is trying to deal with being his daughter's sole parent.

Challenge students to discover the differences in the vocal qualities of an elementary school child, a high school girl, and finally a grown wife and mother. Though the portrayal should not be a caricature, the young actors should strive to convey their ages to the audience. Would the elementary girls speak with slightly higher voices? Would the high school girls speak rapidly and with "high drama," perhaps with slightly lower tones? And how would grown-up moms sound—a little tired after cooking all day and full of Thanksgiving dinner? A little slower? A little lower in tone? Chuckling rather than giggling? Alex's voice should mature over the years somewhat as well. You might suggest that students rehearse with a tape recorder to see if they can capture these vocal changes.

The following words are included in the play. Make sure young actors are familiar with them:

- definitely
- hysterics
- conversation
- calculus
- Valedictorian
- mutual
- mentioned
- scholarship
- uncomfortable
- boutonniere
- permission
- investigate
- professors

Scene 1

As the play begins, we see two stools and music stands, where CINDY and MATTIE sit. ALEX's stool and music stand are stage right, or separated from the other two in some way.)

ALEX Dear Charles,
Well, hi, it's me, your brother Jake who has no idea what he's doing. We've moved into the new house—it's nice, but Mattie really didn't want to leave her friends. I explained to her that I had to move because of my job, and she was brave—but I know she's sad.
Oh, well—we do what we've gotta do, right? I sure do miss Julie, though. I can't believe she's gone. Why on earth did I let her drive that night? It was rainy . . . oh, you know the rest. If she had left five minutes earlier or stayed at home for ten more minutes looking for her keys—but she didn't. She had a wreck, and now I'm all Mattie has. I don't think she blames me, but I don't see how she can help it. Speaking of Mattie, I guess I'd better go find her. She's supposed to be unpacking, but I don't hear her. Anyway, I just wanted to email you and let you know we made it. Write when you have a minute, OK?
Your brother, Alex

CINDY Hello!

MATTIE Who, me?

CINDY Yes, you! My name's Cindy. What's yours?

MATTIE Mattie.

CINDY Do you live here now?

MATTIE Yes. We just moved in.

CINDY I live in this big yellow house. Isn't it ugly?

MATTIE No! It's a beautiful house. Like the one we used to live in.

CINDY I think your new house is pretty.

MATTIE Maybe . . . I miss our old one, though.

CINDY   Do you have your own room?

MATTIE   Yes.

CINDY   Do you have brothers and sisters?

MATTIE   No. Just me.

CINDY   Are your parents nice?

MATTIE   My father's nice, but . . . my mother got killed in a car wreck.

CINDY   That's awful! I never heard anything as bad as that!

MATTIE   I know. I miss her.

CINDY   I bet. Say . . . this fence is between our two houses. I wonder which one of us owns it?

MATTIE   Well—you were here first, so I guess you own it.

CINDY   But it's closer to your house.

MATTIE   Yes, it does seem to be a little closer . . .

CINDY   Let's share it! It isn't yours and it isn't mine—it's ours.

MATTIE   OK. We'll share the fence.

CINDY   And whenever you want to talk to somebody, come down here. Sit for a few minutes, and I'll see you and come out!

MATTIE   You will? You'll come out and talk to me?

CINDY   You bet I will. You've got yourself a friend, Mattie. Am I your first friend since you moved?

MATTIE   Well . . . I did talk to the lady next door . . .

CINDY   Ladies don't count. Am I the first kid?

MATTIE   Yes. You're definitely my first kid friend.

CINDY   Wooo, listen to you! "Definitely!" Are you in high school or something?

MATTIE   No—just sixth *(or insert actor's grade here).*

CINDY   Me too. Sixth *(or insert same grade as MATTIE's)* grade when school starts in the fall.

MATTIE   Are the kids nice in your school?

CINDY   Some are, some aren't. But don't you worry about a thing. You've got good old Cindy for a friend now! Who cares if they're nice or not?

MATTIE   Well . . . I guess you're right!

CINDY   You bet I'm right.

MATTIE   Well—I'd better go in. I'm supposed to be unpacking. I hate my new room. The carpet is this nasty green color.

CINDY   Just pretend that it's the ocean! The ocean looks kinda green when there's seaweed in it.

MATTIE   I've seen the ocean look green before.

CINDY   You bet you have! Just imagine your bedroom carpet has sea horses and fish and maybe a shark!

MATTIE   And a seal! And a dolphin!

CINDY   That's it! Don't worry about that green—just pretend it away.

MATTIE   I will! Well—I've got to go. I'll see you later, OK, Cindy? Will you come out later?

CINDY   If I see you at the fence, I'll come running! Now go unpack some suitcases—and look out for sharks!

(The girls laugh.)

Readers' Theatre

Scene 2

ALEX   Dear Charles,

Just time for a quick note—Saturday's the prom, and Mattie . . . I mean, Matilda—that's what she wants to be called now . . . Matilda's in hysterics. She's got this "boyfriend"—I hate to even say that word. Let me say it like this: There is a boy, and he's Mattie's "friend." There. That's not as obnoxious.

Anyway, they had a fight and they haven't spoken in a few days. The phone rings, she jumps—but it's somebody else. I'm tempted to take the money I spent on a dress, shoes, tanning salon, teeth whitening, and new make-up, and give it to this guy just to get him to call and talk to her. I don't even know what the fight was about. She was trying on her prom dress a few minutes ago and she just started crying and ran out the back door. Kids, huh!

Except for this incident, I have to say that she's doing all right. She's enjoying high school—lots of friends, lots of activities. She wants a car, but I don't know. Seventeen seems so young to be out on the road. Oh, well—I guess I have to let her grow up sooner or later.

I suppose I'd better try to find Mattie . . . excuse me, Matilda . . . and see if she wants to get some dinner. That is, if she hasn't had a better offer . . .

MATTIE   Oh, Cindy, where are you? I need to talk to someone NOW!

CINDY   *(out of breath)* Here I am! I had to run all the way from upstairs! What's wrong?! What are you doing at the fence . . . in your prom dress! Are you crazy?

MATTIE   Yes I am crazy! That's it, Cindy! I'm crazy! I never should have gone on a date with Keith! I should never even have had a conversation with him!

CINDY   Now I know you really are crazy! He's gorgeous! Adorable! Sweet! Nice to his mother! Loves dogs! Should I go on?

MATTIE   I know, I know, that's what's so awful! He is all those things—but we had a fight. It was so stupid . . . he needed help with his calculus. So—who does he call? Sunny Becker! The cutest girl in the school!

CINDY   Sunny Becker? She may be cute, but she's the brainiest kid in school, too! She's in National Honor Society . . . I think she's even the secretary or something . . . and she's sure to be Valedictorian, or at least . . . the other one, whatever it's called.

MATTIE Stop it, OK? I know all about Sunny Becker and how great she is . . . that's why I'm so . . . I hate to say it . . .

MATTIE & CINDY Jealous.

CINDY Mattie . . .

MATTIE Matilda!

CINDY *(sighing)* Matilda. You have got to get a grip. You want Keith to get a good grade in calculus SO he'll graduate in the top ten percent, SO he'll get a scholarship to OU *(insert local university—or "dream" university—here),* and you can go, too, and y'all can get married and live happily ever after . . .

MATTIE Cindy! What are you talking about? I'm not getting married to Keith or anybody else!

CINDY Have it your way. But if you should decide later on that you wanted to marry him, you might like it if he had a job! And you might like it if he had a job that paid a lot of money because he went to college!

MATTIE Oh, I know what you're saying. He should study with somebody smart . . . I just wish it wasn't Sunny! I can see them now . . . sitting at her dining room table, sunlight streaming in the windows . . .

CINDY They're probably sitting on a lumpy, uncomfortable sofa with three dogs and five cats bothering them and making them sneeze . . .

MATTIE And she's saying, "Oh, Keith! You're so smart! And cute, too! Whatever do you see in that old Matilda girl?"

CINDY No, that's not it. Her little brother is hanging on the back of the sofa, going "Sunny is a goober! Sunny is a goober! One time she put salt in her iced tea instead of sugar!" Or something. You know how little brothers have these stories.

MATTIE And he's saying, "Sunny, I never noticed this about you . . . but your eyes are as blue as . . . as the sea . . ."

CINDY   You mean, "Your eyes are as green and ugly as Mattie's carpet in her room."

MATTIE   *(giggling in spite of herself)* Oh . . . I guess I'm being dumb.

CINDY   You are being dumb. Now go in the house and take off that prom dress before it gets grass stains on it.

MATTIE   I will. Oh, Cindy, what would I do without you?

CINDY   You'll never have to find out. You've got yourself a friend, Mattie.

ALEX   Mattie! Matilda! Where are you? Keith's on the phone!

MATTIE   *(shrieking softly)* Aghhh! Keith's calling me! What should I do . . . should I talk to him?

CINDY   Of course. Go ask him what his favorite color is so we can go to the florist and get his boutonniere for the prom.

MATTIE   He'll probably say "Blue, like Sunny's eyes!"

CINDY   *(giggling also)* If he does, you have my permission to hang up—and go to the prom with his friend Glen!

MATTIE   Ew! Glen! I'd rather skip the prom altogether!

ALEX   Mattie! Should I tell him to call back?

MATTIE & CINDY   No!

MATTIE   *(calling loudly)* I'll be right there, Dad!
(to CINDY) Thanks, Cindy. I'll see you later!

CINDY   Brush off your dress! You've got burrs sticking in it!

MATTIE   *(giggling)* Will do! Bye, Cindy! Thanks!

Scene 3

ALEX Hey, Charles!
Happy Thanksgiving! I'm so sorry you couldn't join us this year, but I know that you're having a great time with all your kids and grandkids. Mattie and Glen are here with all three of their little ones—they've grown a foot since I've seen them last. The oldest is the age Mattie was when we moved in here. It's pretty scary how time flies. Anyway, we had a big dinner and now nobody can move, we're so full. Mattie made pies, and we all had to have a slice of each kind. Do you think we'll be able to get together for Christmas? I do hope so. Oops—I think I hear someone crying, and I don't know where Mattie has gotten off to. Better go investigate. Happy Turkey Day! Gobble, gobble!

MATTIE *(to herself)* I will never eat again. I will never eat again. I will never . . .

CINDY Famous last words!

MATTIE Cindy? Is that you?!

CINDY Who else would be at our mutual fence? Happy Thanksgiving!

MATTIE Happy Thanksgiving to you! I didn't think you were going to be able to come home this year!

CINDY I really didn't, either. I didn't think we could afford the airfare. I mean, math professors make a pretty good living, but, as Keith reminds me, "Money doesn't grow on trees."

MATTIE That's for sure! How are the kids?

CINDY Growing too fast, talking too much, driving me crazy. You know—they're great. Tillie is in third grade and Sammy is a first grader. How about yours?

MATTIE Growing too fast, talking too much, driving me crazy. Also great. I think about Mom, though, a lot. Now that I have kids of my own, I really wish she was here to see them. And to help me know what to do, you know?

CINDY Yes, I sure do. I talk to my mother about once a day! I can't imagine raising kids without her help.

MATTIE But Dad's great, and Glen's mother is nice, too. So—I really shouldn't complain.

CINDY Yes, I guess today of all days we should count our blessings. Say, do you want to come over for pie? We haven't had dessert yet. I was just taking out the trash when I heard someone saying, "I'll never eat again."

MATTIE *(laughing)* No, thanks. We've finished pie and every other morsel of food in Dad's house. I think Glen and the kids are lying around like stuffed animals, not able to move.

CINDY OK. Well—I'd better go back in before somebody murders somebody. Hey—do you want to hit some after-Thanksgiving sales tomorrow? Nobody but you was ever crazy enough to go shopping with me on that day!

MATTIE I'd love to! Let me see if Glen and Dad will mind if I leave the kids with them.

CINDY I'll do the same with Keith. Of course we could bring all of them along . . .

MATTIE Hmmm, why don't I think that would be as much fun?

CINDY Maybe we could get our husbands to bring the kids up to the mall to ice-skate when we're through? Then we could all get a pizza or something together?

MATTIE I told you—I'm never eating again!

CINDY And I believed that for about five seconds!

MATTIE That all sounds great, Cindy. Hey . . .

CINDY What?

MATTIE It's good to see you. Thanks for always being at the fence when I needed someone.

CINDY No problem. As I may have mentioned—you've got yourself a friend, Mattie.

(The girls bow their heads.)

ALEX Hello Charles,

It's me again. It was a great Thanksgiving. The house is quiet now—everyone's gone to bed. I just thought I'd send you one more email before I turn in myself. I have a few things planned for the weekend—I have a guy coming over to give me a bid on replacing the fence at the back of the property with a nice wood one. With the little ones running around, I thought it might be good to have a little more security when they visit. I'll ask Mattie what she thinks before she heads out in the morning to shop. Also—I almost hate to mention this, but . . . I met a lady at the grocery store, of all places. She's a widow as well, and we agreed to get together for dinner on Sunday night. I don't know if it will be any huge romance—but maybe just . . . a pal. It would be pretty nice if I could find myself a friend. We'll see. Anyway, goodnight, Brother. And a happy Thanksgiving to you and your family.

(ALEX bows his head.)

At The Fence

Follow-up Activities

1. Girls, think of your best friend. Think about your best friend when she is 18. Think about this same friend when she is married and 28 years old. Write three letters: one to your friend as she is today; one when you're both 18; one when you're both 28 and married, maybe with a child. Though you have no way of knowing for sure, imagine what you'll discuss and how you'll be as older people. (If you can, save the letters somewhere and read them when you really reach that age!)

2. Boys, write a brief paper describing the person you feel is your best friend. Why is he your best friend? Although it's important to share interests and activities, try to think more in terms of how he is as a person. What character traits does he possess that make you want to spend time with him? Try to imagine how he will be when he is a father. In your paper, describe your friend as a dad.

3. The girls in the story meet at the fence. That is their secret and special place. As a class, discuss whether you have a special place to meet your friend. Maybe it's her locker, or maybe it's outside the field house after his football practice. Why did you start meeting there?

4. When *At The Fence* begins, Mattie and her dad have just moved into a new house. The experience of moving into a new neighborhood and trying to make new friends is a tough one for anyone, and one few of us can avoid having to do at least once. Think back to when you moved into your current home. Who was the first person who was kind to you? Who was your first friend? Are you still friends? What was a particularly awful experience that you had soon after you moved? Does it still seem awful, or has your attitude about it changed since? Write a journal entry or short scene about the experience of moving.

5. Choose a short paragraph from your literature book or from some other text. As a class, take turns reading it aloud, first in your own voice, then as a college-age person, then as a grownup, then as someone elderly. As you go through the rest of your day, listen to the voices of the other kids around you, as well as the adults with whom you'll come into contact. Notice how they sound. Notice how mature people use different words than young people, and notice how quickly or slowly they speak.

SOUNDS OF HALLOWEEN

Readers

Sam	Morgan	Mr. Foley
Tera	Alex	Scary Unknown Voice
	Ghostly Chorus	

SOUNDS OF HALLOWEEN

Notes to the Teacher / Director

Prepare for a good fright.

Sounds of Halloween is a spooky play with opportunities not only for good vocal and facial acting and emotion, but for some good scary noise-making as well! The characters Sam, Alex, Tera, and Morgan sneak into the Motley House—known by all to be an honest-to-goodness haunted abode—and get more of a scare than they expected. And every step of the way—as they hear chains rattling, witches laughing, and cats yowling—the Ghostly Chorus is on stage as well, creating the sounds as they hear them. Some of the sounds will be made vocally (such as the sounds of the wind and creaky gate), and some may be made using such props as lengths of chain and blocks of wood. The Ghostly Chorus may be as few as one person or as many as you would like to include. If it's made up of multiple cast members, you may wish to assign certain sounds to certain students. The part of the Scary Unknown Voice can be a member of your Ghostly Chorus (who covers his or her face with the script, perhaps) or it might be fun to have a teacher or the principal deliver this line very loudly, and from offstage.

Encourage your actors to build the suspense for the audience. Imagine how thrilled they'll be if they actually cause the audience to jump or let out little shrieks because they were surprised by a sound! It could happen . . .

The vocabulary in this play is less challenging, but you may wish to review the following words before your cast begins work:

- definitely
- completely
- mournful
- experiment
- myth
- fable
- supposedly
- explanation
- abandoned
- realistic
- mysteriously

Be afraid. Be very afraid.

This play is so much fun . . . it's scary.

(As the play begins, we see at least five stools and music stands. Four are for SAM, TERA, MORGAN, and ALEX, and the rest are for the GHOSTLY CHORUS, which can be as many actors as you wish. The GHOSTLY CHORUS can be set apart from the other four actors, perhaps on the other side of the acting area. Also, if you like, and if possible, the audience may hear recorded spooky sounds as they enter the classroom or performance area. There are notebooks on the music stands. The cast members enter, take their seats on the stools, and open their notebooks. The GHOSTLY CHORUS members either leave their notebooks closed, or bow their heads when they take their seats.)

SAM   Hello, everybody, and happy Halloween! My name is Sam . . .

TERA   And mine's Tera . . .

SAM   That's Morgan . . .

MORGAN   Hello, everybody!

SAM   And that's Alex.

ALEX   Yo, my homies, what is up?

SAM   Alex thinks he's really cool.

ALEX   What do you mean, "thinks"? When you look up "cool" in the dictionary . . .

MORGAN   It says "Not Alex."

ALEX   Well, it sure doesn't say "Morgan."

MORGAN   I think it says "maybe Morgan when she's wearing a new outfit, but definitely never Alex." Yeah, that's what it says for sure.

SAM   So where was I? Oh yes . . . it was last Halloween. Or actually a few days before Halloween. We four learned a lesson we'll never forget.

TERA   It was so-o-o-o-o scary. I'll never forget it for sure.

ALEX   I wasn't scared! I pretended so you girls wouldn't feel wimpy.

MORGAN   Oh really? I think I remember seeing the "swoosh" on your sneakers as you ran past me at the speed of light.

ALEX   Can I help it if I'm the star of the school track team? Even when I'm just strolling—I'm moving!

SAM   We had been to see a Halloween play at our school and we were walking home.

TERA   The play was really funny. It was called *The Scary Contest*. I loved the character named Pillowcase the Ghost.

ALEX   And T-Bone the Skeleton was cool, too. He used a lot of words that started with the letter "T." Hey . . . I guess that's why he was called "T-Bone"!

MORGAN   Nothing gets by you, smart guy!

SAM   Anyway, we were walking home from this play, and it was dark. Because it was, you know, night.

TERA   We didn't usually walk home after dark—usually someone's mother would come and pick us up—but this time our parents said we could walk if we would come straight home.

MORGAN   And none of this would've happened if we had. Gone straight home, I mean.

SAM   See, there's this old house in our town. It's called the Motley House.

MORGAN   Everybody knew that it was haunted.

TERA   We had heard that all our lives. No one exactly knew why it was haunted . . .

SAM   Something about an ancient burial ground . . .

MORGAN   Or an evil scientist . . .

ALEX   Or a crazy seventh-grade teacher *(or insert the grade of your choice)* who started giving pop spelling tests and couldn't stop.

TERA   Whatever had happened there . . . it was haunted. For sure.

SAM   So . . . since Halloween was coming . . . and we were walking home together . . .

MORGAN   And because Alex was a goober and dared me . . .

ALEX I thought YOU dared ME!

MORGAN Really? Maybe I did . . .

SAM Anyway, somehow we got the crazy idea to walk past the Motley House.

TERA Shouldn't have done it.

MORGAN Definitely not.

SAM Here's how it went . . .

TERA The sun was completely down by the time we got out of the play. There was a moon, and it was shining pretty brightly. I mean, even when there wasn't a streetlight, we could see.

MORGAN Do you remember how we looked up and saw a shadow cross the moon . . . ?

SAM But it looked like a witch.

ALEX It WAS a witch. I know a witch when I see one! In fact . . . *(starts to look at the girls)*

MORGAN Oh, Alex, you SO don't want to go there!

TERA It was pretty warm when we started walking, but then a cool wind whipped up.

(For the first time, the GHOSTLY CHORUS members open their notebooks, or raise their heads. They begin to make a faint wind noise. The other cast members don't seem to notice.)

GHOSTLY CHORUS *(wind noise)*

MORGAN I remember dry leaves started to blow past my feet. One got stuck on my sock.

SAM And I remember hearing a cat meowing far away, like it was lost . . .

GHOSTLY CHORUS *(mournful cat sound)*

TERA I remember that cat sound! But I remember that it sounded angry! Like it was about to fight!

Readers' Theatre

GHOSTLY CHORUS	*(angry cat sound)*
MORGAN	When we started walking, there were lots of cars on the road.
GHOSTLY CHORUS	*(car sounds, including engines, horns honking, and ad libs such as "Get out of the way, buddy!" and "Hey, slow down!")*
ALEX	But the farther from school we got, the quieter it got. Soon it seemed as if there was no one out except us.
TERA	I remember trying to talk the others out of going to the Motley House. "Guys," I said, "we should get on home. Our parents will be worried!"
SAM	"We won't be that much later," I said. "Just ten minutes or so. Then we'll go straight home."
MORGAN	I said that it would be fun. A scary Halloween thing to do.
ALEX	And then you dared me to go . . .
MORGAN	I still think it was you. Anyway—we decided to go for it.
SAM	We walked along quietly for a few minutes. Then—there it was.
ALEX	The Motley House.
TERA	I'm scared all over again!
MORGAN	"Come on, Tera," I said. "Be brave. Let's show them what girls are really made of."
SAM	We walked up to the gate. We stood there and looked at it. An owl hooted.
GHOSTLY CHORUS	*(owl hoot sound)*
	(They jump.)
TERA	We all jumped.
MORGAN	Then we laughed at ourselves. You know, nervous laughter.
ALEX	I was the one to say it first. I said, "Let's go in."
TERA	I thought he was crazy. I said, "Are you crazy? That's the Motley House! It's almost Halloween! We can't go in there!"

SAM	Let's just try the gate. It's probably locked.
MORGAN	Sam pushed the gate . . .
GHOSTLY CHORUS	*(sound of squeaky gate)*
MORGAN	And it opened.
SAM	We all stood there for a minute, looking at each other. I know I was waiting for someone to be first—to actually step through the gate and walk up to the house.
MORGAN	I kinda wanted it to be me . . .
TERA	I knew it wasn't going to be me . . .
ALEX	It was me. "Come on," I said, leading the way. "Last one on the porch is a . . . a rotten jack-o-lantern."
SAM	We walked onto the porch and peered in the windows. Cobwebs were everywhere. I thought I heard spiders . . . making spider noises.
GHOSTLY CHORUS	*(little "chittery chittery" sounds like a spider might make. This can be a verbal sound, or experiment with rubbing paper, cloth, or kitchen sponges together.)*
MORGAN	Spiders don't make any noise!
SAM	I heard spider noises!
GHOSTLY CHORUS	*(repeats spider sounds)*
SAM	In fact . . . I almost think . . . *(acting as if he might be hearing the GHOSTLY CHORUS now)* . . . oh, never mind. Back to the story . . .
ALEX	I was brave and walked right up to the door. I put my hand on the knob.
TERA	Alex, don't! I'm scared!
ALEX	Come on, Tera! Don't be silly! This house isn't haunted! It's just an old wives' tale. Just a myth! Just a fable!
MORGAN	The door is probably locked tighter than a drum. Nobody's going inside . . .

Readers' Theatre

GHOSTLY CHORUS	*("scree" sound of squeaky door opening)*
SAM	The door! It opened by itself!
TERA	Alex, you did that! You gave it a push!
ALEX	Uh . . . I don't think so, Tera. It just opened . . . by itself . . .
SAM	You know what, guys? This is getting weird. I wonder if we should get out of here . . .
MORGAN	Oh come on, Sam, don't be a sissy! If Tera and I are brave enough to go in this supposedly haunted house, then you must be. And look . . . here I go . . .
SAM	Morgan walked right in through the front door. The rest of us looked at each other . . . gulped . . . and followed her inside.
ALEX	I wasn't really scared at all. My dad builds houses, and so I knew that there was a perfectly good explanation. Maybe the foundation of the house was uneven . . . or the floor was warped . . . or maybe the wind blew the door open . . .
TERA	But then . . . do you know what happened next? We were creeping into the living room of this old house . . . quietly . . . tiptoeing . . .
GHOSTLY CHORUS	*(loud door slamming sound—either a big vocal "Bam!" or slamming of two pieces of wood together.)*
MORGAN & TERA	*(letting out little screams)* The door! It slammed shut!
ALEX	It was the wind, I tell you. Come on. We've come this far . . .
SAM	Alex led the way. We took little steps, staying pretty close together.
GHOSTLY CHORUS	*(mad cat sound again)*
TERA	That sounds like the cat we heard earlier! Only now it sounds like it's in here! With us!
MORGAN	Don't be silly. Cats all sound the same . . .
GHOSTLY CHORUS	*(mad cat sound again)*

TERA	But that one sounds really mad . . . and really close . . .
ALEX	Guys! Look! There's a staircase! And look! There's a candle . . . holder . . . thingy . . . with candles burning!
TERA	This is getting really creepy. Why would candles be lit in this abandoned old house? I don't like this one bit.
MORGAN	I think it's cool! Somebody's probably celebrating Halloween a little bit early! I bet we find some . . . Eagle Scouts upstairs. Let's go see.
SAM	Morgan started for the stairs, but no one seemed to want to follow. In fact, Tera said:
TERA	No way. I'm not going up those stairs. In fact, I'm leaving. Anybody who wants to escape this spook house, come with me!
SAM	Tera ran for the door, wrapped both hands around the knob, and pulled it. Hard. And . . .
TERA	Nothing happened! Guys . . . this door isn't budging! We're trapped!
SAM	We were all getting a little jumpy, when all of a sudden . . .
GHOSTLY CHORUS	*(cackling witch laugh)*
MORGAN	Did you guys hear that? A laugh?
ALEX	This just gets cooler by the minute! Let's go check out what the Eagle Scout thought was so funny!
SAM	We didn't know what to do. At least I didn't.
TERA	I didn't either! I mean, I was scared to death and wanted to leave . . . but the door was locked.
MORGAN	I was a little scared, I'll admit . . . but I really wanted to see who was in that house, lighting candles and laughing . . . well, like a witch!
ALEX	I wasn't confused. I wanted to go up those stairs and have an adventure! "Come on," I said. "Let's go solve this mystery."
SAM	The girls linked arms . . . and, in a minute, I linked arms with

	Tera, I'll confess. With Alex in the lead, we walked slowly toward the staircase.
MORGAN	We thought we heard a rat . . .
GHOSTLY CHORUS	*(rat-like "eee-eee" sounds)*
TERA	And we heard that mad cat again . . .
GHOSTLY CHORUS	*(mad cat sounds)*
ALEX	But still we went up . . . and up . . . and up the stairs . . .
SAM	And when we got almost to the top . . . a puff of wind blew through the house, snuffing out the little flames on the candles!
GHOSTLY CHORUS	*(wind sounds)*
	(a pause, then:)
MORGAN	We were in the dark.
TERA	Now we all four linked arms, held hands, grabbed onto belt loops . . . whatever we could find to tie us together. And for some reason . . .
SAM	We kept climbing those stairs.
ALEX	It was awesome.
MORGAN	When we got to the top, we were all shaking in our sneakers. Our ears were alert for any sound we might hear, anything to warn us that danger was near. As we listened, we heard a far-away, faint sound . . .
GHOSTLY CHORUS	*(soft sounds of chains clanking)*
SAM	It started softly, then got louder . . .
GHOSTLY CHORUS	*(louder chain sounds)*
TERA	Guys? Do you hear that?
MORGAN	Probably just somebody's snow chains . . . on their car . . .
ALEX	Snow chains? We live in Florida! *(or insert warm-climate place here)*

SAM	The sound of chains grew louder and louder . . .
GHOSTLY CHORUS	*(loud chain sounds)*
SAM	We held our ears and braced ourselves for something coming around the corner, something with chains hanging on it . . .
TERA	When, just as suddenly as it had come—it stopped.
GHOSTLY CHORUS	*(chain sounds stop)*
MORGAN	We breathed a sigh of relief . . .
SAM, TERA, MORGAN, ALEX	*(sighing)*
MORGAN	. . . and then we saw a little light down a hallway. We didn't talk about it—we just started walking toward it.
SAM	The other spooky sounds didn't stop. We heard a squeaky door close . . .
GHOSTLY CHORUS	*(squeak, then slam)*
ALEX	And we heard more sounds like, you know, critters . . .
GHOSTLY CHORUS	*(sounds of skittery spiders, and rat squeaks)*
MORGAN	And just when we got to the end of the hall . . .
TERA	Where we had seen the faint light . . .
SAM	We heard a really ghostly, scary wail . . .
GHOSTLY CHORUS	*(ghostly "Wooooooo" sound)*
ALEX	OK! That will be quite enough!
SAM	Alex broke into a run, toward the light. We all tore after him—believe me, nobody wanted to be alone at that point.
MORGAN	We got to the door, and I grabbed the knob. I pulled it with all my might!
TERA	It opened. We could see someone . . . or something . . . in the far corner of the room.

Readers' Theatre

SOUNDS OF HALLOWEEN *(Script pg 10)*

SAM   Alex called out:

ALEX   Hello? Excuse us!

SAM   But there was no answer.

MORGAN   I joined in. "Hello!" I called. "Answer us!"

SAM   Still there was no reply. We started walking toward him . . . or it . . .

TERA   Now the sounds were really getting loud. *(As the following sounds are described, the GHOSTLY CHORUS makes them.)* Rats screeched . . . cats yowled . . . doors slammed . . . chains rattled . . . witches cackled . . . and that awful mournful wail continued on and on . . . until we got up to the creature who was bent over what looked like a table, with a lot of lights . . .

ALEX   Our hearts were pounding, but we walked up to him . . . or it . . .

SAM   We shouted to be heard over the racket.

MORGAN   *(shouting)* Sir! Excuse us! Hey! Whatever you are!

SAM   The noises continued. The . . . creature . . . didn't answer us. So Alex reached out and touched its shoulder . . .

(MR. FOLEY opens his notebook, raises his head, or one of the GHOSTLY CHORUS becomes MR. FOLEY. As all the other eerie noises stop abruptly, MR. FOLEY jumps, startled, and lets out a frightened cry.)

MR. FOLEY   Ahhh! For Pete's sake! Scare me to death, why don't cha!

TERA   What . . . who . . . are you?

MR. FOLEY   My name is Ken Foley. And who are the four of you? And how did you get in here? That front door sticks so badly!

ALEX   I'm Alex. This is Tera . . . and Morgan . . . and Sam. What are you doing? Why didn't you answer us?

MR. FOLEY   I didn't hear you because of these headphones. *(He pantomimes taking headphones off of his ears.)* And as for what I'm doing . . . why, I'm recording scary Halloween sounds for a CD! I'm thinking about calling it "Scary Halloween Sounds." What do you think?

Readers' Theatre   ©2006 by Incentive Publications, Inc., Nashville, TN

MORGAN	Wait a minute. You're recording spooky sounds?
MR. FOLEY	Yes!
SAM	So all those chains and witches and cats . . . that was all you?
MR. FOLEY	Well, I didn't think I had the volume up that loud, but I guess so. See my recorder? It's state-of-the-art!
ALEX	Yeah, that looks pretty neat . . . but why here? Why aren't you in a recording studio or someplace?
MR. FOLEY	Well, I will finish things up at a real recording studio. But as for why I'm here . . . where better to record spooky sounds than in a real honest-to-goodness haunted house?
MORGAN	Do you really think it's haunted?
MR. FOLEY	*(laughing)* I wish! No, kids, I'm just teasing you. I thought there might be some neat squeaky floors or windy chimneys in this old house . . . but the scary sounds were all mine. I was just trying to get a few more noises to add!
ALEX	Cool! We were really scared for a minute there!
SAM	I'd say longer than a minute . . .
TERA	We were completely spooked. Your scary sounds were very realistic!
MR. FOLEY	Really? They sounded . . . real?
ALEX	Reel . . . to reel!

(Everybody laughs.)

MORGAN	Well, everyone, it has been "reel." But I think we had better scram out of here, let Mr. Foley finish his CD, and get home before we get in all kinds of trouble!
ALEX	To think we were tricked like that! I can't believe it! We all thought those sounds were honest-to-goodness ghosts and ghouls! I think we should come back here on Halloween night. Yeah, that would be great! Let's have a party right here . . .
SCARY UNKNOWN VOICE	Woooo! Get . . . out . . . of . . . my . . . house!

Readers' Theatre

MR. FOLEY, ALEX, TERA, MORGAN, SAM	_(screaming)_ Ahhhhh!
TERA	Needless to say, we ran like the wind.
MORGAN	Including Mr. Foley.
SAM	The front door was mysteriously standing open when we got downstairs, and we flew down the porch steps like we were on fire. When we got home, we were all late and we all got grounded and we didn't get to have any fun on Halloween night.
TERA	So the moral of this story is . . .
MORGAN	Go home when you're supposed to.
ALEX	And don't go in haunted houses or any other abandoned buildings.
SAM	There could have been a stray dog in that old house or some person who might have hurt us, so we shouldn't have gone in. But, of course . . . it wasn't really haunted!
SCARY UNKNOWN VOICE	Or . . . was . . . it?
ALL	Ahhhh! Happy Halloween, everybody! Be safe and careful!

Sounds of Halloween

Follow-up Activities

1. Write a short, two-person scene between two ghosts who live in the Motley House. You may wish to include dialogue about how tired they are of having people intrude, how they look forward to Halloween, the scariest sounds they make, etc. Though the play is done in readers' theatre style without costume or make-up, perform this scene with ghostly rags for clothing and white make-up with dark circles under your eyes. Or—be stereotypical ghosts and cut eyeholes in white sheets. It might be fun to add a pair of glasses outside the sheet or perhaps a belt around the waist of one of the ghouls.

2. As a last-part-of-the-day activity on a Friday before Halloween, have the cast or class members bring flashlights to school, sit in a circle, shine the flashlights into their faces, and tell ghost stories. Plan the activity for a couple of days so students have time to remember the stories and have them ready to share.

3. In the early days of radio, there were shows broadcast which relied on sound effects in order to create the mood for the audience. A famous story is H.G. Wells's *War of the Worlds,* which created a fictitious alien invasion—just before Halloween. See if you can find a recording of the original broadcast, which was so believable it threw the nation into a state of panic. As you listen to it, see if you can imagine what was used to create the sound effects. At least two movies have been made based on the story; rent and watch one as a class if you like, but remember that the original story was told only by voices and sound effects.

4. If there is a recording studio within field-trip distance of your school, see if you can visit. If you can arrange for a tour, ask the technician to demonstrate how sound effects are made in modern recordings.

5. Take a scary story such as those in the Goosebumps novels for young readers, and adapt it for performance. Would it lend itself to readers' theatre? Are there scenes that could be described more easily than they could actually be performed? Perform it for the class, either as a scene with blocking, or as readers' theatre.

The Great Science Fair Tragedy

Readers

Chorus

Leader of the Chorus

The Principal

Toby-ocles

Agamem-mom

Cassandra

Toby-ocles's Brother

The Great Science Fair Tragedy

Notes to the Teacher / Director

Although there are differences of opinion as to how the art form known as "theatre" began, all seem to agree that the ancient Greeks played a major role. Initially, these festivals were religious in nature, intended to ensure fertile land and fertile people. Greek citizens would gather out of doors to watch plays in the huge open-air theatres (from the word theatron or "seeing place"). In early theatrical offerings, audience members were standing when they watched the performances; later, stadium-like seating became available. The area on which the acting took place was "raked"—that is, the back portion of the stage was physically higher than the front portion, thereby allowing the spectators greater visibility. (The terms "upstage" and "downstage" had their beginnings in Greek theatre. The area at the back of the stage was, literally, "up.")

The chorus was an integral part of the Greek theatrical experience. A large group of performers, chanting and singing, served to narrate and move the action along in the play. In all the roles, much emphasis was placed on the actors' voices; a clear, pleasant and the ability to portray a full range of emotion were of top priority. Some early Greek plays covered actors' faces entirely with masks, relying upon voice and physical movement to convey the story and emotions.

The Great Science Fair Tragedy is actually more comedy than tragedy, and utilizes that Greek convention of the Chorus. In our play, the Chorus does not sing or dance, but simply reads its lines as one entity. As in ancient Greece, the Chorus is very important in this play. Cast as many young people as you would like to include, making sure to allow enough rehearsal time for them to be able to read their lines in unison.

As with other plays in this collection, there is opportunity to personalize the play with your city's name, principal's name, and grade level.

This is a tongue-in-cheek offering which sticks Greek-sounding suffixes on the ends of modern names to make them sound Greek (except for Cassandra, whose name sounds plenty Greek as it is). Make sure you pronounce "Toby-ocles" as "Toby O'Cleeze" rather than "Toby Ockles." (Somehow that just doesn't have the same Greek ring to it . . .)

Make sure your cast knows the meanings and pronounciations of the following words and phrases which may be new to them:

- minimum
- supported
- digestion
- deciduous
- catalpa

- mistreated
- disqualified
- desperate
- mirth
- lactose intolerant

- decree
- fluorescent
- competition
- resemble

Here is a theatrical footnote: In ancient Greece, men played all the parts—even those which were female. There is, however, no need to be quite that historically accurate. Surely Sophocles and Aeschylus won't mind too much if girls take part in your production!

*(Chairs and music stands for the CHORUS members are to one side
of the acting area at an angle. Chairs and music stands for the rest of the cast
are arranged facing the audience. As the play begins, actors' heads are bowed;
they raise them as they speak for the first time.)*

CHORUS Welcome one, welcome all!
Come and join us for this tale;
A story of woe, a story of grades, a story of the science fair.

LEADER OF THE CHORUS Perhaps these good people, these citizens of _____ *(Insert your
city's name.)*, do not know the meaning of the word "woe."

CHORUS Can this be true?
Have your lives been so happy, people of _____, that you know
not the meaning of "woe"?

LEADER OF THE CHORUS We will help you to understand. This is woe:

CHORUS *(wails and cries and falls around dramatically; then stops abruptly)*

LEADER OF THE CHORUS That was also an example of "overacting."

CHORUS Never mind us.
Tell these good people about Toby-oclese.
Tell them about the lesson he learned.

LEADER OF THE CHORUS Let us start at the beginning.

CHORUS That's a very good place to start.
When you read, you begin with A-B-C.
When you sing you begin with do-re-mi.

LEADER OF THE CHORUS Cease! This is a Greek-style play,
Not *The Sound of Music*.

CHORUS We are sorry.

LEADER OF THE CHORUS Here is the principal, Mr. Peters-chylus. *(Or, insert the name of your
principal here and stick "chylus" on the end of his name. Not only will
his name have a Greek sound, but it will also sound like "kill us," which
may reflect some students' ideas of what their principal is trying to do.)*

THE PRINCIPAL *(raising his head)* Yes, it is I.
I am the principal of this school.
It is my duty to make sure each and every student learns
all he or she can.

Readers' Theatre

It is my duty to make sure that mystery meat is served
in the cafeteria.
It is my duty to make sure that fun is kept to a minimum.

CHORUS   That is a principal, all right.

THE PRINCIPAL   Once again, it is time for my favorite day of the year.

CHORUS   Report card day?

THE PRINCIPAL   No.

CHORUS   Open house?

THE PRINCIPAL   No

CHORUS   Eye exam day?

THE PRINCIPAL   Back off, Chorus.

CHORUS   We are sorry.

THE PRINCIPAL   Here is my decree:
On this day, all students in the school will be required
to think and to plan.
They will do research, speak to their teachers,
speak to their parents.
They will visit the library and decide on the
all-important, difficult-to-complete . . .
SCIENCE FAIR PROJECT.

CHORUS   Oh, woe to the student body!
Woe to the boys and girls who would rather be riding their bikes
Or playing soccer
Or watching television.
Woe to the parents who will have to help with ideas,
To take kids to the library,
To buy those three-fold pieces of poster board!
But woe, woe, especially woe to . . .
Toby-ocles, a _____th-grade boy. *(Insert grade level here)*

TOBY-OCLES   *(raising his head and looking miserable)* I'm afraid that's me.

THE PRINCIPAL   I'm expecting great things from Toby-ocles this year.

Readers' Theatre

104

TOBY-OCLES	Woe is totally me.
THE PRINCIPAL	That is because his brother, the best student ever to grace these halls . . .
TOBY-OCLES	Here it comes.
THE PRINCIPAL	The older brother of Toby-ocles WON THE SCIENCE FAIR FOR THE WHOLE CITY OF ATHENS . . . er, I mean _____ *(insert your city here)* . . .
TOBY-OCLES & THE PRINCIPAL	Three years in a row!
CHORUS	Poor, poor Toby-ocles! Whatever shall he do? What hope can he have of living up to the great legend of his brother? Should he quit school? Should he pretend to be sick? Should he ask his parents to move to a neighboring town?
TOBY-OCLES	Chorus, you are not helping.
CHORUS	Again . . . we are sorry.
TOBY-OCLES	But they are tragically right! My brother made history in this school. In science fairs through the years, he amazed student and teacher alike.
CHORUS	Tell us, Toby-ocles! What did he do? What did he make?
TOBY-OCLES	One year, he made a small engine that was powered by ground-up milk cartons.
CHORUS	Oooooooh!
TOBY-OCLES	He also invented dry water, so that no one would ever need to own a towel.
CHORUS	Ahhhhhh!
TOBY-OCLES	He even invented a cure for the common cold—but he was disqualified. The judges thought our parents must have helped him.

Readers' Theatre

CHORUS　What a shame.

TOBY-OCLES　And now, here I come.
Following in his footsteps.
Or rather—trying to jump from one of his huge footprints
to the next without falling and breaking my pitiful neck!
But I am weak!
I am puny!
I am not up to the challenge!

CHORUS　You are right.

THE PRINCIPAL　Nonsense, Toby-ocles!
You are your brother's brother.
You have the same parents! You must have the same talents!
That's the way this stuff works.

TOBY-OCLES　But Principal Peters-chylus, I fear that is not so!
I am a pretty decent goalie,
And I can multiply and divide without using my fingers,
And I can draw well enough so that people know what
my picture is supposed to be.
But I am not my brother!
And he is not I!

CHORUS　Thank the gods!

THE PRINCIPAL　No matter what you may say about your brother,
The time for the science fair is upon us.
You must have your project ready in two weeks!

CHORUS　Two weeks, two weeks!
That is very little time!
How can Toby-ocles think of a project at all,
Much less get it done!
Things look very hopeless.
Things look very dark.
Things look very bleak . . .

TOBY-OCLES　Have the members of the chorus ever heard of self-esteem?
For mine is taking a beating.

CHORUS　Go home, Toby-ocles!
Go home to your mother!
Go home to a dinner of pot roast, asparagus, and pork n' beans!
Your cousin Cassandra has come to visit!

TOBY-OCLES	Oh, no.
AGAMEM-MOM	*(raising her head)* Suppertime!
TOBY-OCLES	Hello, Agamem-Mom.
AGAMEM-MOM	Hello, Toby-ocles. Come, and tell me stories! Tell me tales of your adventures! Let me revel in the glories of your day at school! Eat your pot roast.
TOBY-OCLES	What's Cassandra doing here?
CASSANDRA	I, Cassandra, your cousin Have come to dinner for reasons known only unto my own parents. Something about a chariot race that they wanted to attend . . .
TOBY-OCLES	A chariot race?
CASSANDRA	Maybe it was NASCAR.
AGAMEM-MOM	Both of you must hush, now, and enjoy your food. I have spent many hours in preparation of your evening meal. You must not talk of things that will upset you, or your digestion will not be good. So—Toby-ocles—I hear it's science fair time again.
CHORUS	Woe to Toby-ocles! Woe to his digestive system!
TOBY-OCLES	It's true, Agamem-mom. It is time for me to try my hand in the arena in which my brother was so successful. I must create a project.
CASSANDRA	Oh, dear cousin, give it up! You can't hope to compete with your brother! He had many victories in science competition!
TOBY-OCLES	Yes, Cassandra, but he is away at college now.
CASSANDRA	Indeed, he is away at the University of Hecuba . . .
CHORUS	One "heck-uva" school!

Readers' Theatre

CASSANDRA	But you cannot hope to do as well!
TOBY-OCLES	Yet—I must try. And . . . I almost hate to say it . . . I have an idea.
CHORUS	Tell us, tell us! What is your plan? Will you rise to your brother's challenge? Will you bring home the gold medal?
TOBY-OCLES	I want to grow ivy in different kinds of water And different kinds of light.

(A long silence, then everyone onstage bursts out laughing.)

AGAMEM-MOM	Now stop, everyone! Hold your mirth! Although it seems like a foolish idea for a project . . . it is my son's idea! Well—not my older son . . .
CHORUS	Who won many science fairs . . .
AGAMEM-MOM	And who had a free ride to the University of Hecuba . . .
CHORUS	What a scholar!
AGAMEM-MOM	But my younger son, my Toby-ocles Who has come up with an . . . interesting idea . . . for the science fair.
CASSANDRA	What do you mean, different kinds of water? What do you mean, different kinds of light?
TOBY-OCLES	Why would I try to explain? You all mock me—no one has my back!
CHORUS	Poor Toby-ocles! He feels mistreated!
TOBY-OCLES	Well, not mistreated exactly . . . But certainly not supported!
CHORUS	Poor Toby-ocles! He feels let down, like the fallen arch of a foot!

TOBY-OCLES	I'm going to work on my project! And I'm going to win! My own idea is just as good as my brother's! You will see! All of you will see!
LEADER OF THE CHORUS	So time passed. A fortnight came and went.
CHORUS	How long is a fortnight?
LEADER OF THE CHORUS	I have never known. A long time, I am sure. Toby-ocles gathered water from the kitchen faucet.
TOBY-OCLES	I'll show them! I'll show them all. Here is kitchen faucet water in a baby-food jar.
CHORUS	He also gathered water from a neighbor's pond.
TOBY-OCLES	This is green! Ivy will flourish.
CHORUS	He filled a baby-food jar with bottled water.
TOBY-OCLES	Sparklets!
CHORUS	And finally, water from an old boot he found next to the family garage.
TOBY-OCLES	Yuck! This could certainly have bred mosquitoes!
LEADER OF THE CHORUS	He went to the ivy which was growing on the side of the house And there he cut four pieces, which he placed in his baby-food jars of water.
TOBY-OCLES	Let me see . . . I will put the kitchen faucet water under the fluorescent light in the kitchen . . .
CHORUS	Grow little ivy, grow!
TOBY-OCLES	And this pond-water ivy will go in the yard, under a tree.
CHORUS	Help Toby-ocles to avoid disgrace!
TOBY-OCLES	The Sparklets will go in a window on the back of the house.

CHORUS   Will he win? Will he fail?

TOBY-OCLES   And this water from the old boot will come to rest in a window on the front of the house, in this empty bedroom.

CHORUS   Good luck to Toby-ocles!
May the ivy grow and help him avoid embarrassment and ruin!

TOBY-OCLES   We will see what we will see.

CHORUS   Every day he visited the ivy.
Every day it looked just the same.
Toby-ocles began to worry.

TOBY-OCLES   I'm beginning to worry.

CHORUS   Time was passing.

TOBY-OCLES   I'm running out of time.

CHORUS   He began to fear that he had made a mistake.

TOBY-OCLES   I'm afraid I made a mistake.
What was I thinking? I cannot do what my brother did!
Maybe I can think of something else to try . . .

CHORUS   Toby-ocles thought and he thought.
He chewed his bottom lip the way people do
when they're thinking.

TOBY-OCLES   Ow!

CHORUS   He chewed too hard.

TOBY-OCLES   Maybe I can cut a corner . . . wait! Cut! That's it!

CHORUS   Toby-ocles had an idea, but it wasn't very honest.

TOBY-OCLES   Desperate times call for desperate measures!
I remember a science fair project I saw once . . .
Many kinds of leaves had been gathered and labeled.
There were simple leaves, compound leaves,
Some were called deciduous . . .
Some were flat, some were hollow . . .
There were many kinds of leaves.

CHORUS	Will you do the same project, Toby-ocles? Will you gather many leaves from many trees?
TOBY-OCLES	I would like to do this . . . And yet I fear I have no time! I know what I can do . . .
CHORUS	Oh no, Toby-ocles, do not become dishonest!
TOBY-OCLES	But I must! Time is short! I will gather a lot of leaves from the same tree And cut them to resemble other leaves! It will not be honest, but maybe I can turn my project in on time!
CHORUS	But what about your ivy? Will you give up?
TOBY-OCLES	I will not throw it away or pour out the water. I will leave the baby-food jars where they are. But I have not seen any change yet And time is running out. Off I go to collect leaves!
CHORUS	So Toby-ocles journeyed to his back yard. He searched for just the right leaf for his trickery.
TOBY-OCLES	Here we are! These leaves from a tree known as catalpa are large in size! They can be fashioned into many other leaves with the aid of scissors.
CHORUS	No, Toby-ocles! Do not cut the leaves with scissors! Even if you win, it will not be an honest victory!
TOBY-OCLES	Quiet, Chorus! "Leaf" me alone!
CHORUS	Did he say "leaf"?
LEADER OF THE CHORUS	I am afraid that was his line.
CHORUS	Oh, woe be unto the Chorus for having to hear such a corny joke from Toby-ocles! "Leaf me alone." What a terrible pun!

Readers' Theatre

TOBY-OCLES   There! I have finished!
The leaves are cut, mounted on poster board, and labeled
with a Sharpie.
I will present it to my mother for her critique.

AGAMEM-MOM   Toby-ocles! What brings you to the kitchen table
at this hour of the night?

TOBY-OCLES   Behold, Agamem-mom!
I have saved face.
Though my ivy project was a failure, I have collected
various kinds of leaves!
See? They are mounted and labeled.

AGAMEM-MOM   Hmmm . . . let me see.
Why Toby-ocles, this is wonderful!
This is educational and interesting!
Wait a minute, my son. What's this?
Toby-ocles, this leaf has zigzag edges . . . it is cut with
scrap-booking scissors!
Did you cut these leaves to make them appear to be different?

TOBY-OCLES   I cannot tell a lie, Agamem-mom.
I did.

AGAMEM-MOM   This is a disgrace.
You cannot enter the science fair with a fake project!

TOBY-OCLES   But I . . .

AGAMEM-MOM   I do not want to hear your excuse.
You had better create an honest science fair project
Before the sun comes up tomorrow.

TOBY-OCLES   Yes, Agamem-mom.
Say . . . did she say something about the sun coming up?
That gives me an idea . . .

CHORUS   What is Toby-ocles thinking?
Why is he running upstairs?
Is he thinking that he will jump out the window to avoid
the science fair?

TOBY-OCLES   No, Chorus!
I have remembered that one of these baby-food jars of ivy

Has been placed on the east side of the house,
where the sun comes up!
And look!
It has sprouted roots and is twice as big as the other ivy!
My first idea has worked after all!

CHORUS Glory to Toby-ocles!
Glory to ivy!
Glory to eastern sun!

TOBY-OCLES Glory to rubber cement, so I can use the same poster board again!

LEADER OF THE CHORUS Toby-ocles worked late into the evening.
He wrote about his conclusions.
He gathered the ivy together on a tray.
He mounted pictures that he had taken daily.
He redid his poster board.
He left a note for his mother . . .

TOBY-OCLES I am leaving a note for my mother.
It says, "I have raced to school early to set up my project."

CHORUS He raced to school early the next day to set up his project.

THE PRINCIPAL What a glorious morning!
The day I've lived for!
I will walk among the science fair projects arranged
on the gym floor
And see which ones are the winners.

CHORUS Which projects will the principal choose?

THE PRINCIPAL Hmmm . . . a project about being lactose intolerant . . .
interesting . . .

CHORUS Oh, good principal! Please visit the project of Toby-ocles!

THE PRINCIPAL Here is a collection of seeds . . . tidy, but boring.

CHORUS What about this project? What about the ivy?

THE PRINCIPAL Hmmm . . . cure for the common cold again!
Bunch of cheaters . . .
Say! What is this?

TOBY-OCLES   It is my project, sir.
I grew ivy from the same plant in different kinds of water
And different kinds of light.

THE PRINCIPAL   Hmmm. I see that you did.
And this ivy is decidedly bigger and has more roots
than the rest!

TOBY-OCLES   Yes, sir!

AGAMEM-MOM   Toby-ocles!
I got your note! I came as quickly as I could!

THE PRINCIPAL   Why, Toby-ocles . . . I do think you have an interesting
project here!

TOBY-OCLES   Really?

THE PRINCIPAL   Yes, I do. What kind of water did you say you used
for this big one?
And what kind of light?

TOBY-OCLES   Water from an old boot beside our garage at home.

AGAMEM-MOM   Why, that's your brother's old boot!

TOBY-OCLES   And light from the east side of the house.

AGAMEM-MOM   And that's your brother's old bedroom!

THE PRINCIPAL   Why, Toby-ocles!
Using your brother's boot water and his bedroom window,
you have done it!
You have managed to win first place in the science fair!
I might say your brother won this for you,
And he isn't even here!

TOBY-OCLES   Well, yes . . . you might say that . . .

CHORUS   We would not say that, Toby-ocles!
You did it all yourself!
You did not know the boot belonged to your brother!
And so what if that was his old bedroom?
It was your project, and you won fair and square!

TOBY-OCLES Thank you, Chorus!
For once I completely agree with you!

CHORUS No problem-o.

AGAMEM-MOM I'm so proud of you, Toby-ocles!
You did it!

CHORUS Way to go, Toby-ocles!
You're the champ!

THE PRINCIPAL Congratulations, young man!
Your brother would be so proud!

TOBY-OCLES'S BROTHER I am proud!
I am here to say so!

CHORUS Who is this?
Who is in the gym with the science fair projects?

TOBY-OCLES'S BROTHER It is I, Toby-ocles's brother.
It is a student holiday at my university, so I came here
to support my brother.

CASSANDRA And I have come also!
It is not a student holiday at my school!
I am absent-without-leave.
I hope someone will write me a note.

CHORUS What a glorious day!
Toby-ocles has won, and is surrounded by loved ones!

TOBY-OCLES I am happy to see you all!
And I have learned a lesson today.
You have to be true to yourself
And do your own work.
You can't compare yourself to someone great
who has come before you.
And—it doesn't matter where the boot water came from.
It is still your ivy.

TOBY-OCLES'S BROTHER Principal, what's he talking about?

THE PRINCIPAL I don't know, son. It's all Greek to me.

CHORUS   Boo, boo, what a terrible pun!
Now our production is quite done.
Though our hero had a close call
It wasn't a tragedy after all.
We thank you for coming to the play
And wish you all an award-winning day!
Goodbye!

Follow-up Activities

1. At the library or on the Internet, do some research about Greek Theatre. Divide up the following topics, write a paragraph defining and describing each, and share with the class.

   - Buskins
   - Euripides
   - Functions of the Greek chorus
   - Deus ex machina
   - Dionysus
   - Antigone

   - Thespis
   - Satyr plays
   - Kordax
   - Comedy
   - Parados
   - Tunics

   - Sophocles
   - Choregoi
   - Skene
   - Tragedy
   - The Trojan Women

2. Using your research, write a variety of words and phrases that deal with Greek theatre on slips of paper, divide the class into two teams, and play Greek Charades, acting out the Greek terms on the slips of paper. (You can include the ones in #1, above.) Keep time— each student has only three minutes in which to act out his or her Greek word or phrase. The team with the shortest total time wins.

3. Though this play is comedic in nature, it does deal with some issues that some of us must face, such as the overachieving older sibling. If you have such a brother or sister, write a short paper describing how you feel about him or her—both good and bad. If you are the overachiever, discuss how you relate to your younger sibling (or friends, if you have no sisters or brothers). Discuss the pressures put on you by your situation, and how your parents, teachers, or friends help (or could help) you to deal with the stress.

4. Another theme in the play is that of being honest. When Toby-ocles is tempted to snip the leaves into the shapes he needs, he is considering taking a shortcut that will help him save face. As a class, discuss situations to which you've been exposed in which you have observed someone else behaving in this way, or been tempted to take such a step yourself. Discuss why this is a really good idea—or a really bad idea. What might result?

5. Write a brief Greek-style scene about a recent event, such as an important football game, a dance, a great new movie, a hard homework assignment, etc. Include two or three characters and a chorus. As a class, choose the best three and present them as readers' theatre offerings. Or—make masks, wear bedsheet tunics, and perform the short scenes for the rest of the class as they Greeks did in ancient times.

6. Many Greek plays were performed with masks, with actors relying on their voices and physical movements to portray their characters. Just for fun, make a mask of your own face and hang it with your fellow actors' masks around the room. Use creative materials, such as steel wool for hair, sequins for eyes, red licorice strips for your mouth. Invite another class into your room to see if the members can guess which mask goes with which student.

Four Seasons of Fun

Readers

Boys	Girls
One Boy	One Girl
Second Boy	Second Girl
Two Boys	Two Girls
Three Boys	Three Girls

Four Seasons of Fun

Notes to the Teacher / Director:

Here is a light-hearted romp through the four seasons of the year, celebrating the images and ideas that make each special.

Lines divisions and assignments between Boys, Girls, and solo Boys and Girls are suggestions only. Feel free to appropriate the lines any way you like—or let your cast decide. As your cast practices reading this poem/play, note the rhythm of the words per season. It starts with springy, upbeat images of spring, then moves to longer lines, slower delivery—ahhh, summer. The autumn portion features a more rhythmic, rhyming order to the verses, reflecting the return to structure that school represents. As your students move into the winter portion, the tension builds . . . the lines start with single speakers, adding another and one more as the excitement increases, much as it does in homes everywhere in December. Then, all join in for the joyous final lines, celebrating together the fact that there is, truly, something to celebrate around every corner.

Encourage your young speakers to play with the sounds of the lines. For instance, they should hold the "Sssss" sound at the beginning of "sssssummertime," setting the stage for the lazy pace of the summer months—and the lines ahead.

Or course, personalize the line about the Pirates football team to reflect your own mighty, fighting gridiron stars.

Though readers' theatre actors traditionally dress in black, you may want to break with tradition and have your actors dress to represent each of the four seasons. Have two or three girls, for instance, wearing springy Easter-like dresses, while two or three boys dress in sweaters for the fall.

Have fun, and enjoy the four seasons of the year. Each one truly does have its own unique charm.

GIRLS Spring!

BOYS Spring!

ALL Spriiiiiiinnnnnnggggg!

GIRLS There's a bounce in our steps.

BOYS There's a bloom on the walk.

GIRLS There's a bud on the tree.

ALL It must be spring!

GIRLS Wind blows, birds sing.

BOYS Sun shines, bells ring.

GIRLS Wait—what bells ring?

BOYS What can we say? We wanted a rhyme!

GIRLS Better luck next time . . .

ALL Pink and green and yellow and blue,

GIRLS Bunnies and baby goats, fresh and new.

BOYS Awwww . . . look at the babies!

ALL Tulips and irises, white lilies too;

GIRLS Tender colors, kissed with dew.

BOYS Clouds drift lightly up above.

GIRLS Young men's thoughts turn to love!

BOYS Yuck! Not ours!

BOYS Not hot yet; it's still just right.

GIRLS Rainy days and chilly nights.

BOYS Summer's just around the bend;

GIRLS Go outside and find a friend . . .

ALL   It's spring!

GIRLS   Then . . . one day . . . you'll look about
And notice that your school is out . . .

BOYS   Aw shucks! We were having soooooo much fun . . .

ALL   Summer . . . sssssssssssummertime!
Lazy days . . .sssssssssssummertime!

BOYS   Slow down, take off your shoes,

GIRLS   Fill your glass with tea . . .

BOYS   And fun! Let's run!

ALL   It's sssssssssummertime.

ALL   The big, hot sun toasts lazy days, soooooo bright.

GIRLS   Little fireflies polka-dot the night.
The sunflower peeks up over the gate.

BOYS   Summer is here! Let's stay up late!

ALL   Picnics in the park or your own backyard;

GIRLS   Don't forget to make a Father's Day card!

BOYS   Bring all your lawn chairs and meet at the park;
There's a baseball game until it's dark.

GIRLS   (Or maybe longer if they turn on the lights!)

BOYS   Watermelon slices, lots of juice,

GIRLS   Eat outside! Don't swallow the seeds, my dears!
You don't want a vine to grow out your ears!

BOYS   Let's drink cold soda from a bucket of ice,
And eat drumsticks from the ice cream truck.

ALL   Cook hot dogs on the grill, spitting and plumping;
Pass the mustard, pass the ketchup,

GIRLS   Give me pickles, give me relish.

Readers' Theatre

122

BOYS	I relish the relish!
GIRLS	Oooh, that was bad . . .
BOYS	Is there a hamburger?
GIRLS	Just one left!
ALL	How we love the good, good tastes of sssssssummertime!
ONE BOY	Public pool,
SECOND BOY	Belly flops,
ONE GIRL	Fourth of July,
SECOND GIRL	Fireworks pop;
GIRLS	Bikes and friends and summer showers;
BOYS	We'll run and sweat and play for hours. School? Don't say that word! What a bummer!
GIRLS	We'll study later;
ALL	For now, it's sssssssssummer!
GIRLS	But wait? What's that? A little breeze . . .
BOYS	What has happened to the trees?
GIRLS	The leaves were green, but now they're red, Fluttering down upon our heads.
BOYS	Build a pile, use a rake,
GIRLS	Then put it away, for goodness sake!
BOYS	Run and jump and dive right in!
GIRLS	Time to greet a golden friend.
ALL	Summer was great, we had a ball; But now it's time to welcome fall!
BOYS	Back to school!

Readers' Theatre

GIRLS   Oh well, new shoes!
And friends to tell us all the news.

BOYS   Football games on Friday night;
Awesome! Watch those Pirates fight!

GIRLS   Marching band is always great.
New show at half-time! We can't wait!

BOYS   We weren't thinking about the weather,

GIRLS   But all at once we need a sweater!

ALL   At the stadium, feel the north breeze;
Wrap a blanket around your knees.

ALL   There's something magic in the air.
Cats and ghosts give us a scare.

BOYS   Look at that witch! Her skin is green!

GIRLS   Trick or treat!

ALL   It's Halloween!
Green and orange, black and gold;

GIRLS   Stories of ancestors, days of old;

BOYS   Turkey, cranberries, we stop and pray;

ALL   And count our blessings; Thanksgiving Day.

ALL   Then . . .

ONE GIRL   In the stores

TWO GIRLS   And on TV;

GIRLS   Something that we start to see . . .

ONE BOY   Shiny red

TWO BOYS   And also green;

BOYS   Can it be that time again?

TWO GIRLS	Silver bells Ring loud and clear
GIRLS	Holiday time is almost here!
TWO GIRLS	Snow flutters
GIRLS	Drifting down A soft, white blanket across the town.
TWO BOYS	Cookies, candy,
TWO GIRLS	Holiday lists; All these gifts!
TWO BOYS	Whom did we miss?
THREE BOYS	School's out, A little break,
THREE GIRLS	Lots of tasty goodies to bake.
BOYS	So hard to wait!
GIRLS	Can't wait to see
ALL	What gifts there are for you and me.
GIRLS	We jump in bed That winter's night, While snow is falling deep and white
BOYS	Say, what's that sound? It can't be true! Sleigh bells and stomping reindeer hooves?
GIRLS	Fly down the stairs, But don't make a sound! A man dressed in red; his belly is round!
BOYS	"Wait! No way!"
GIRLS	You say in a hurry.
BOYS	"That guy is just a man in a story!"

BOYS	"He's not the real deal. I'll bet you a dollar That's just my old dad in a white furry collar!"
ONE BOY	"Excuse me, there, son,"
GIRLS	Says dad's voice from upstairs.
ONE BOY *(same)*	"If I'm way up here—how can I be there?"
ALL	December is magic! Of that there's no doubt So do like the song says and don't ever pout!
GIRLS	Ring! Ring!
ALL	Riiiiiiiinnnnngggg out the old! And bring Baby New Year in out of the cold!
ALL	The year will unwind, day after day;
ONE BOY	With colors
ONE GIRL	And laughter,
ANOTHER GIRL	And Valentine's Day.
ONE BOY	And throughout it all, one thing is just great
ALL	There's always something to celebrate! Thank you for coming! Have a wonderful year!

Four Seasons of Fun

Follow-up Activities

1. Prior to your performance, have an art day in class. Using finger paints, map colors, or crayons, have your cast members create art to represent the four seasons that they will bring to mind with their voices. Assign several students per season, or divide the poster board or paper into four sections and have each section represent a season. You may also wish to utilize scrapbooking supplies—stickers, notions, buttons, and other three-dimensional items—instead of sticking with crayons or markers. Give your students several days notice so they can begin to collect items at home or even outside. Post their artwork on the day of their performance.

2. Ask your students to search through their CD collections and find music that reminds them of each of the four seasons. Winter / Christmas should be easily acquired—but what songs feel like spring? Like summer? The selections will surely be different from student to student, and there certainly aren't any right or wrong choices. Ask a student to compile all the music into one "pre-show" CD to play while the audience enters. Or, consider timing a recording so that the a spring song plays softly under the spring portion of the play, etc.

3. Have your students write one-page papers describing their favorite season. Remind them to include sounds, colors, smells, favorite foods and to describe the season as though the reader has never experienced it before. Read the papers aloud or create your own *Four Seasons of Fun* reading from your students' work!